JAPAN Coloring Book

Discover These Pages That Kids Can Complete For Fun

No part of this book may be reproduced or used in any way or form or by any means whether electronic or mechanical, this means that you cannot record or photocopy any material ideas or tips that are provided in this book.

Copyright 2019

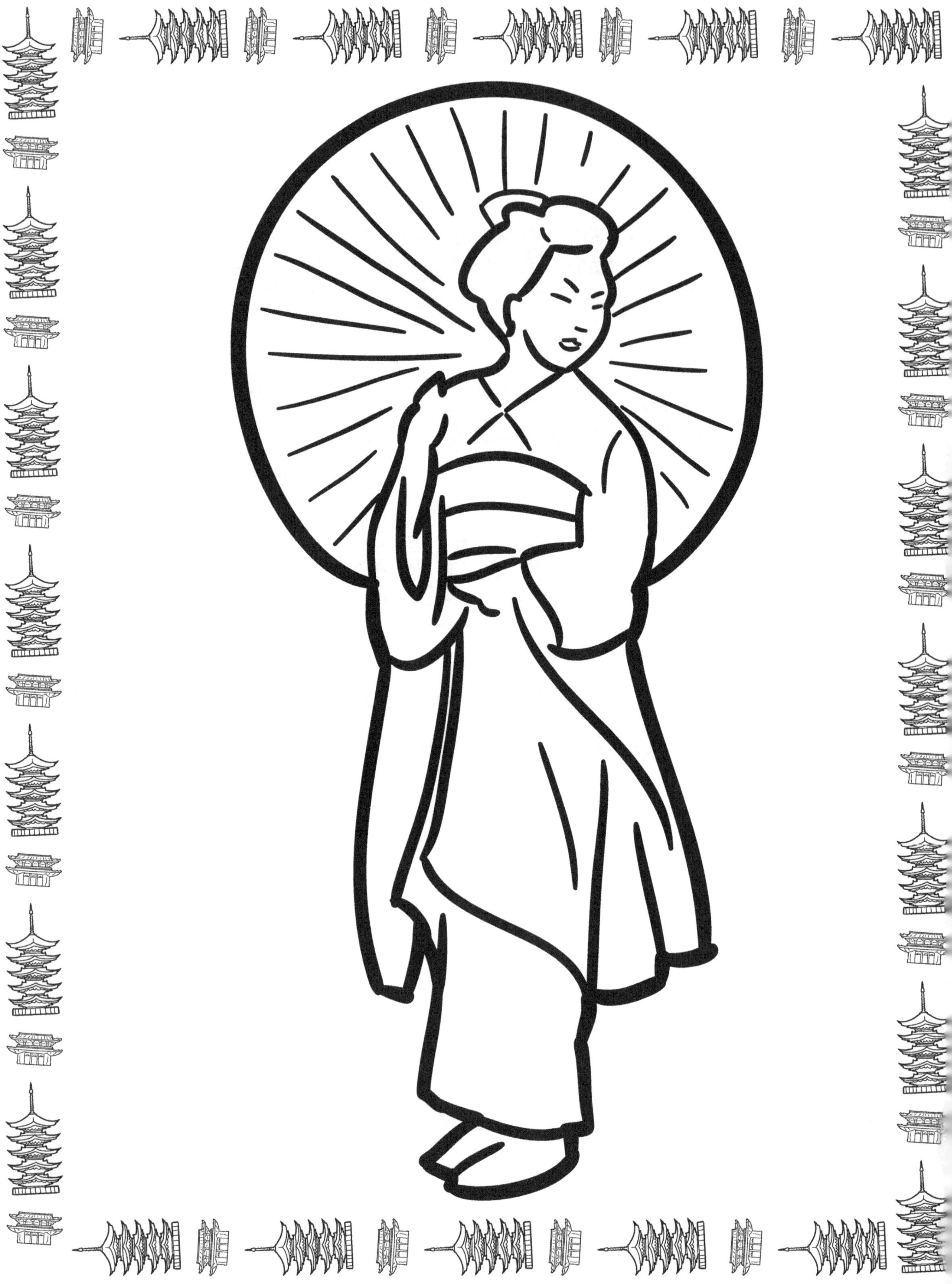

This is a Bleed Through Page If You Are Using a Coloring Marker or Pen!

Bold Illustrations
COLORING BOOKS

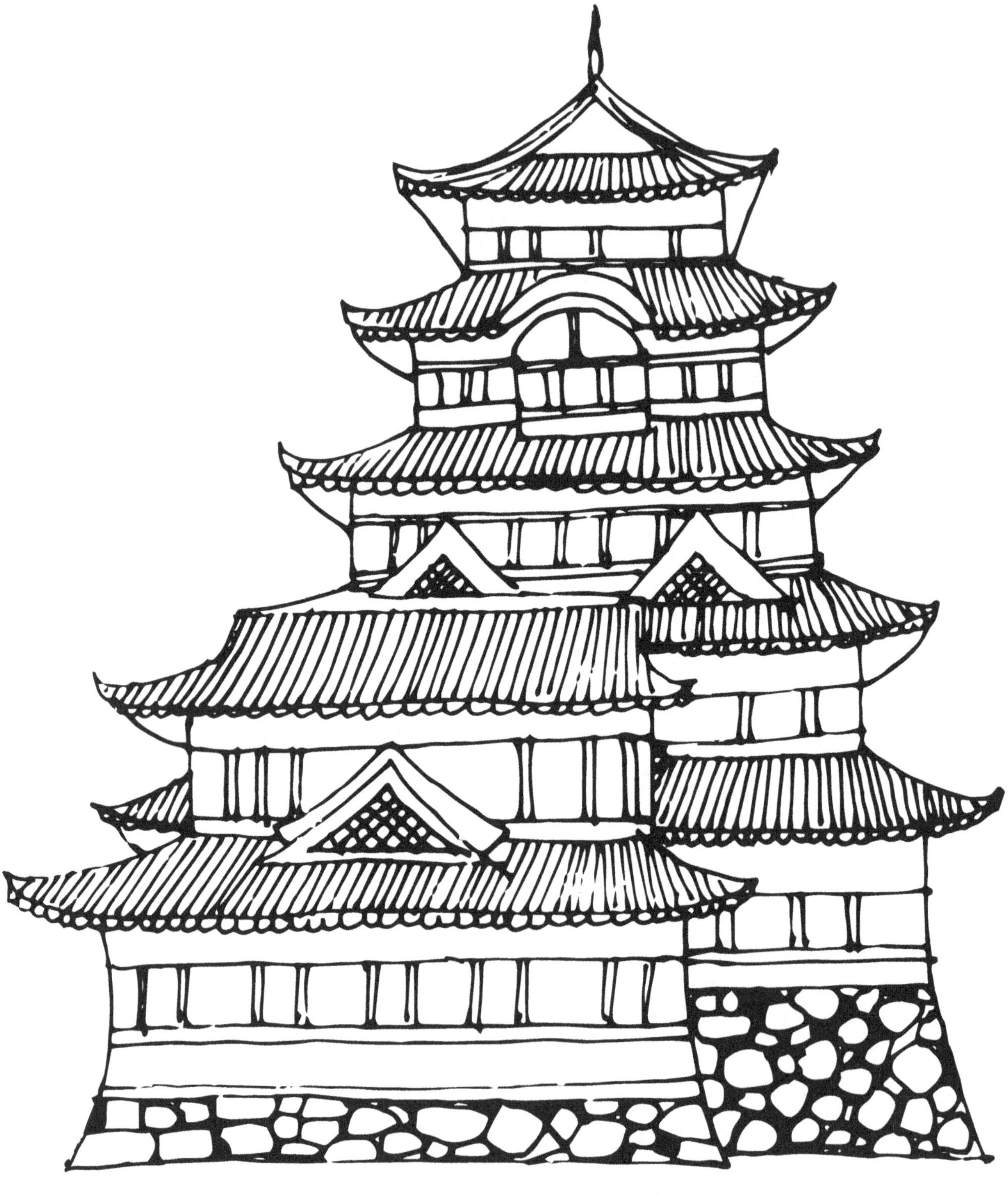

This is a Bleed Through Page If You Are Using a Coloring Marker or Pen!

Bold Illustrations
COLORING BOOKS

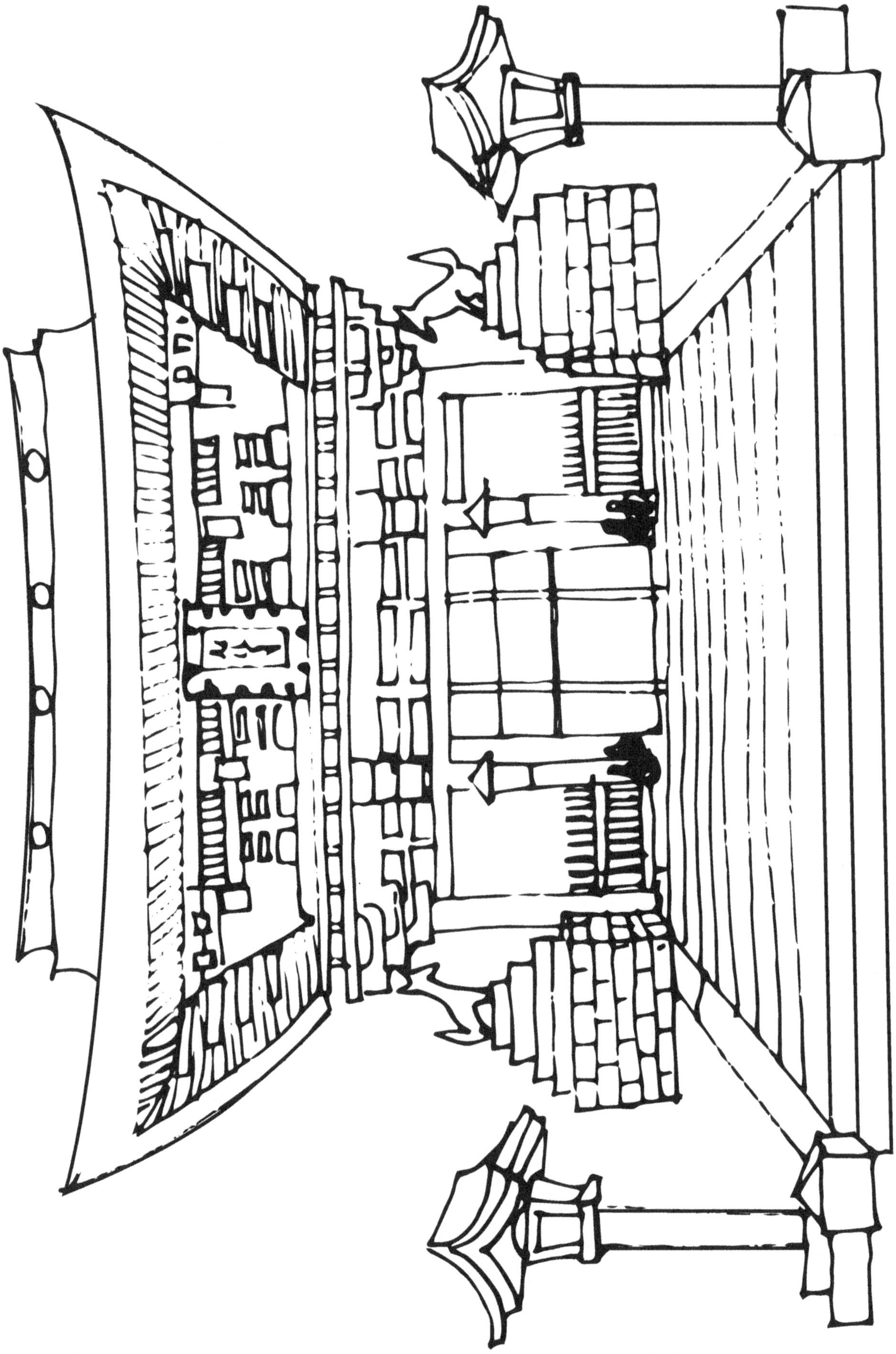

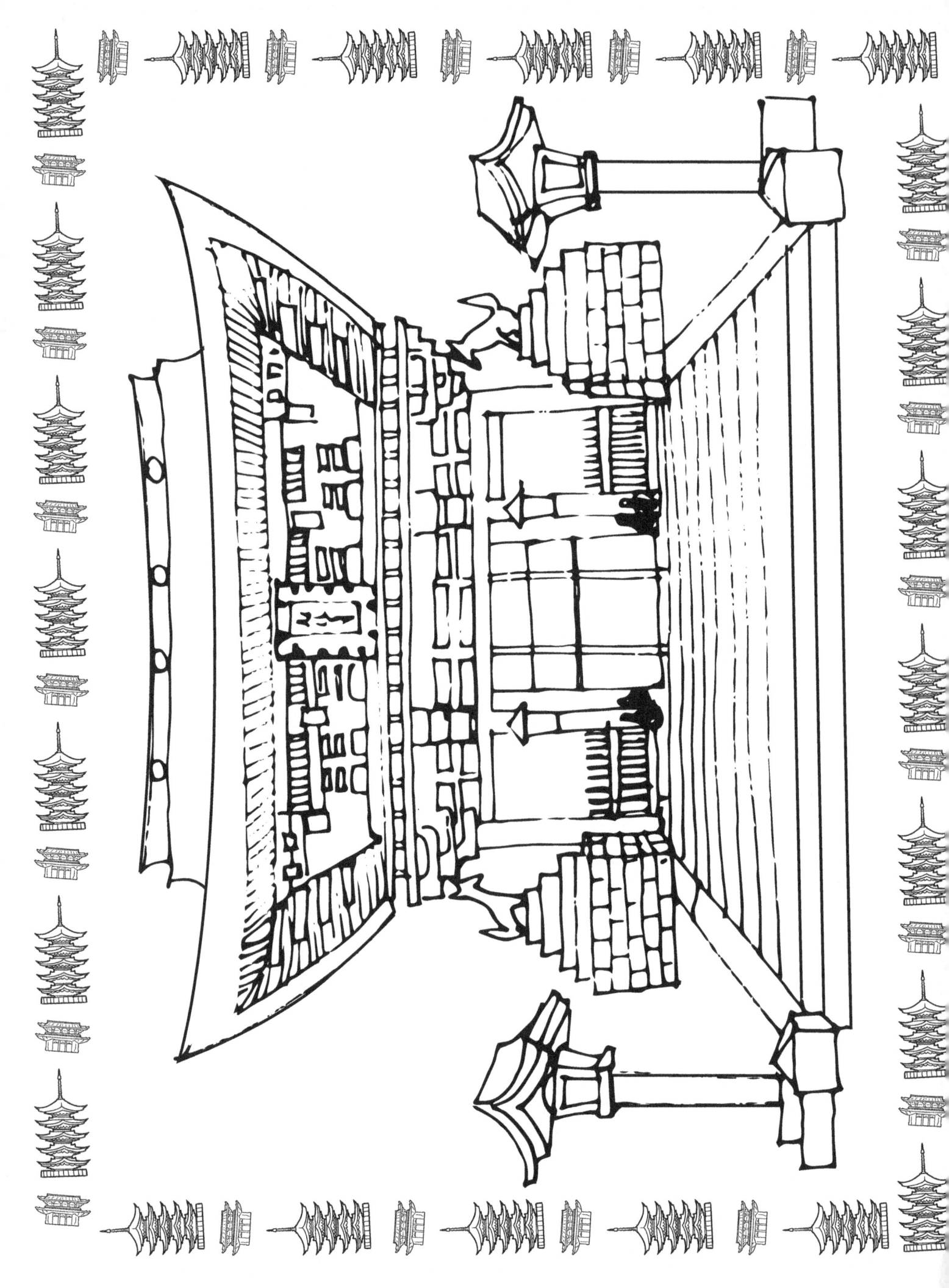

This is a Bleed Through Page If You Are Using a Coloring Marker or Pen!

Bold Illustrations
COLORING BOOKS

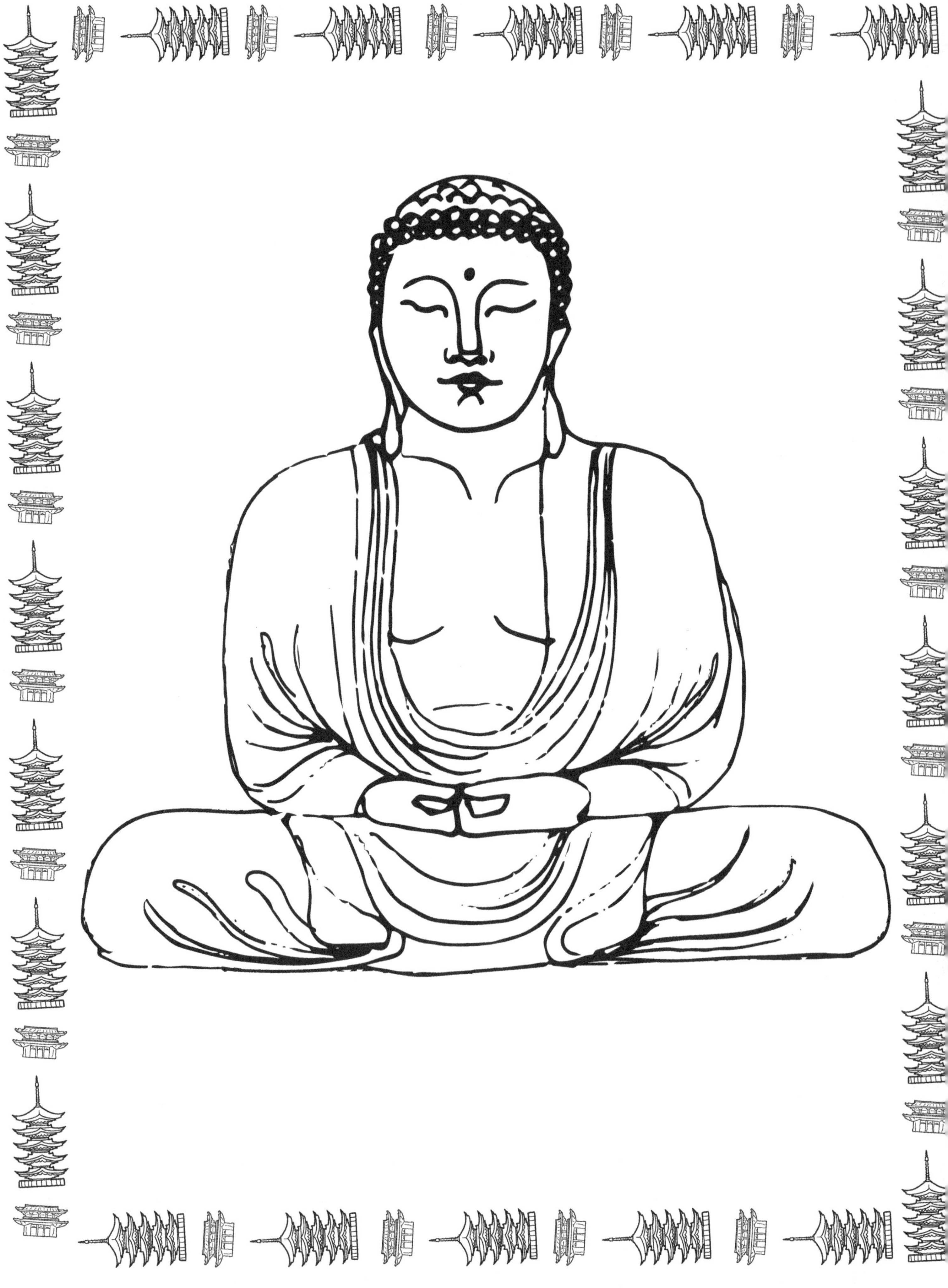

This is a Bleed Through Page If You Are Using a Coloring Marker or Pen!

Bold Illustrations
COLORING BOOKS

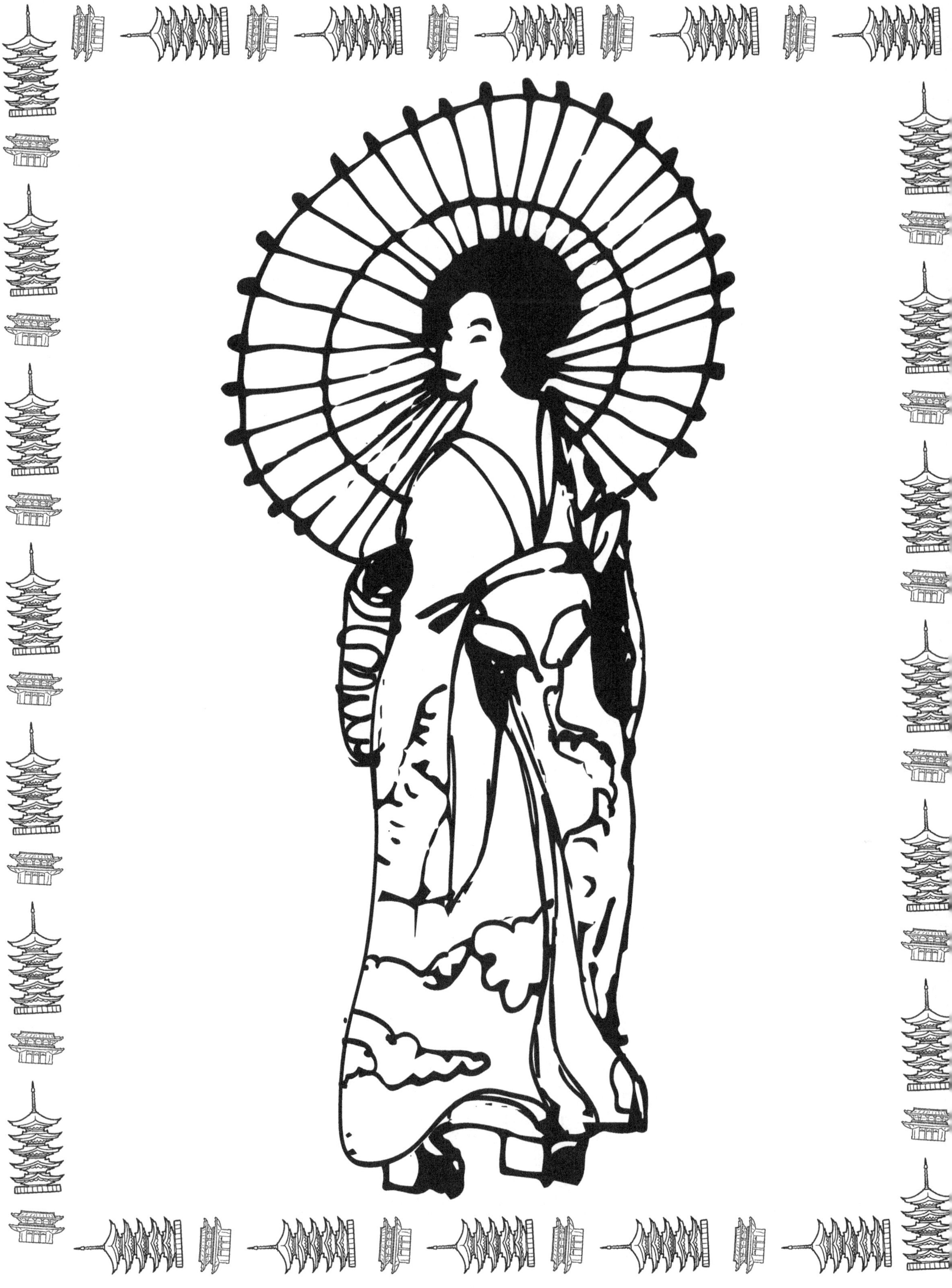

This is a Bleed Through Page If You Are Using a Coloring Marker or Pen!

Bold Illustrations
COLORING BOOKS

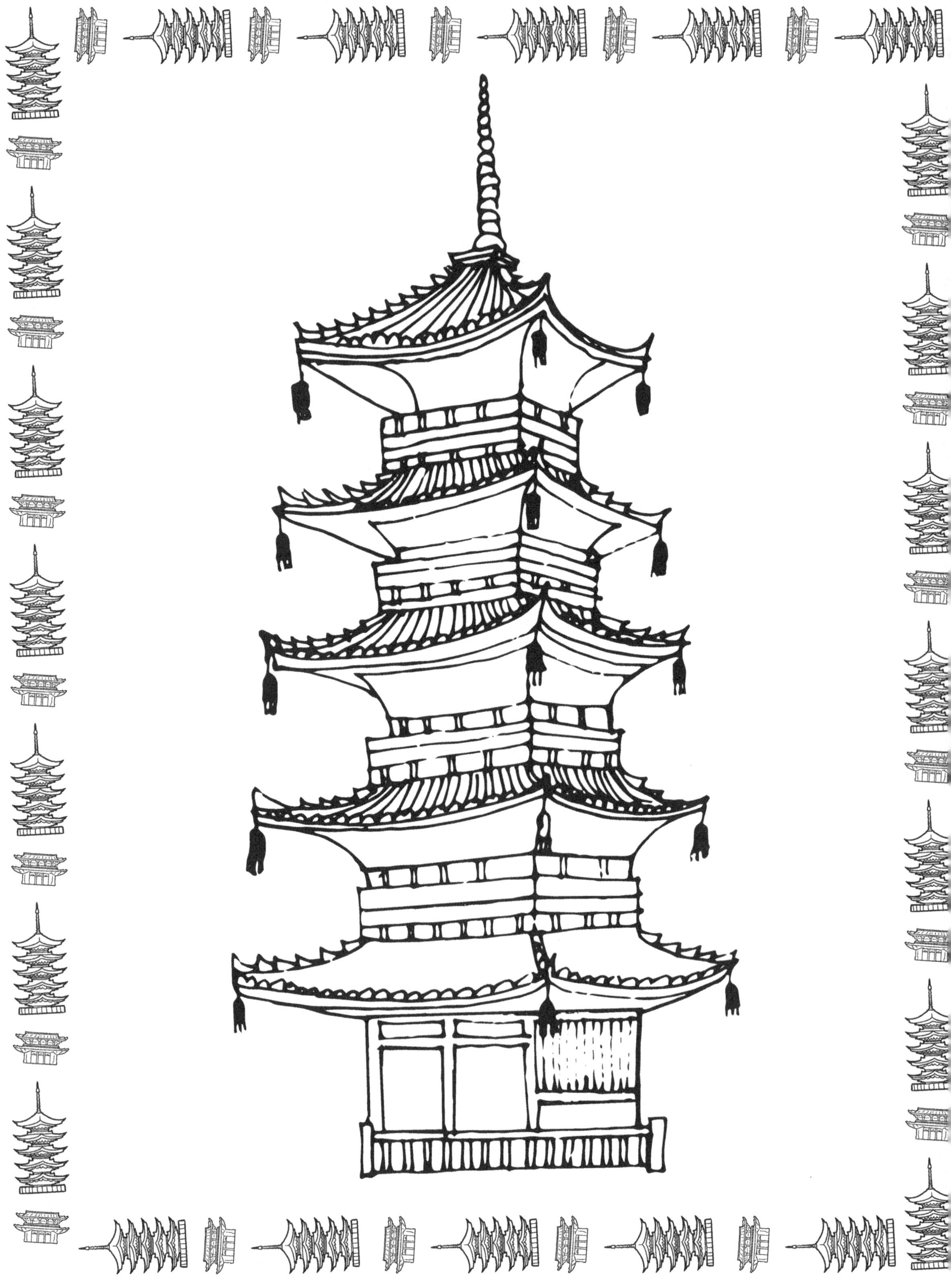

This is a Bleed Through Page If You Are Using a Coloring Marker or Pen!

Bold Illustrations
COLORING BOOKS

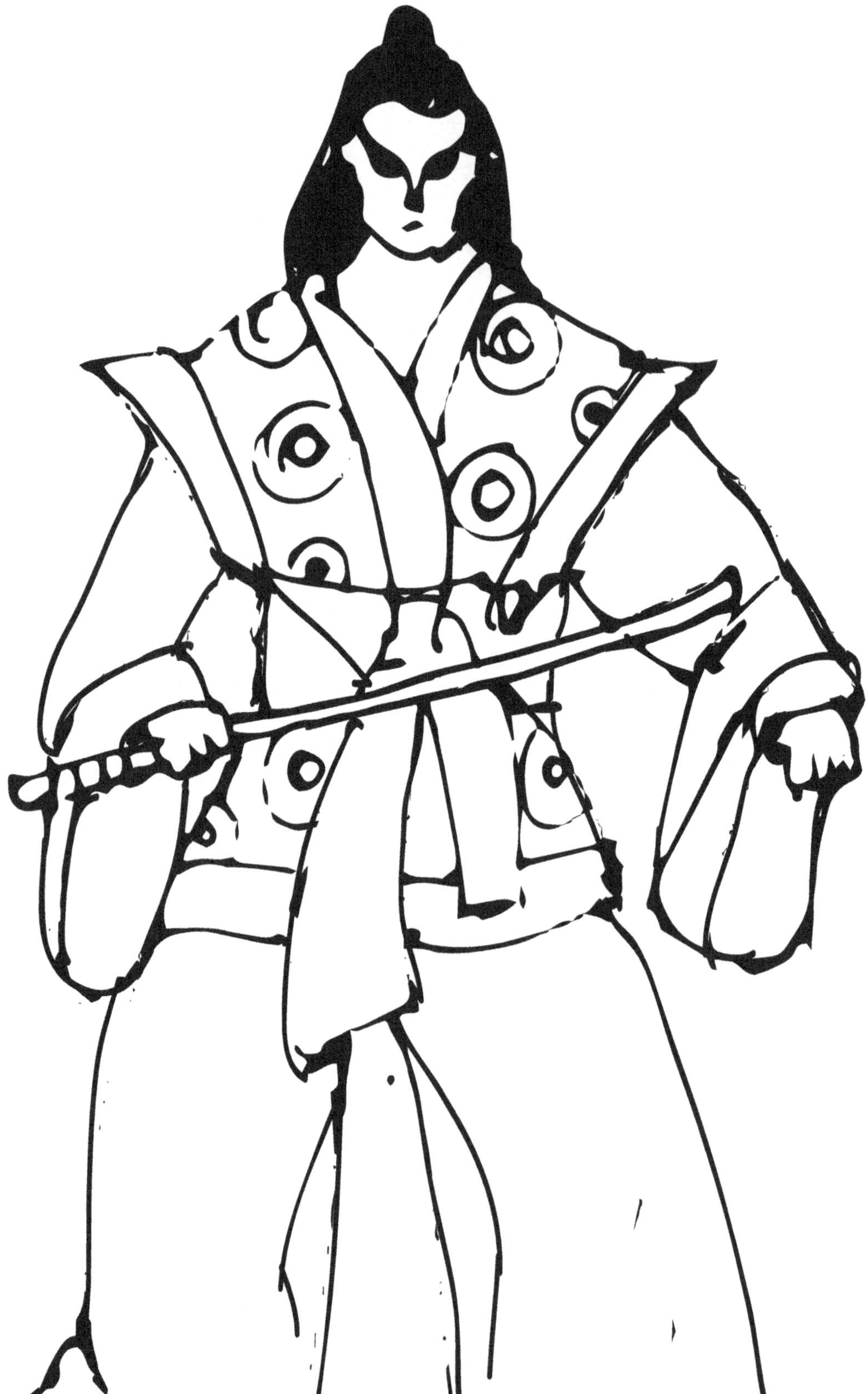

This is a Bleed Through Page If You Are Using a Coloring Marker or Pen!

Bold Illustrations
COLORING BOOKS

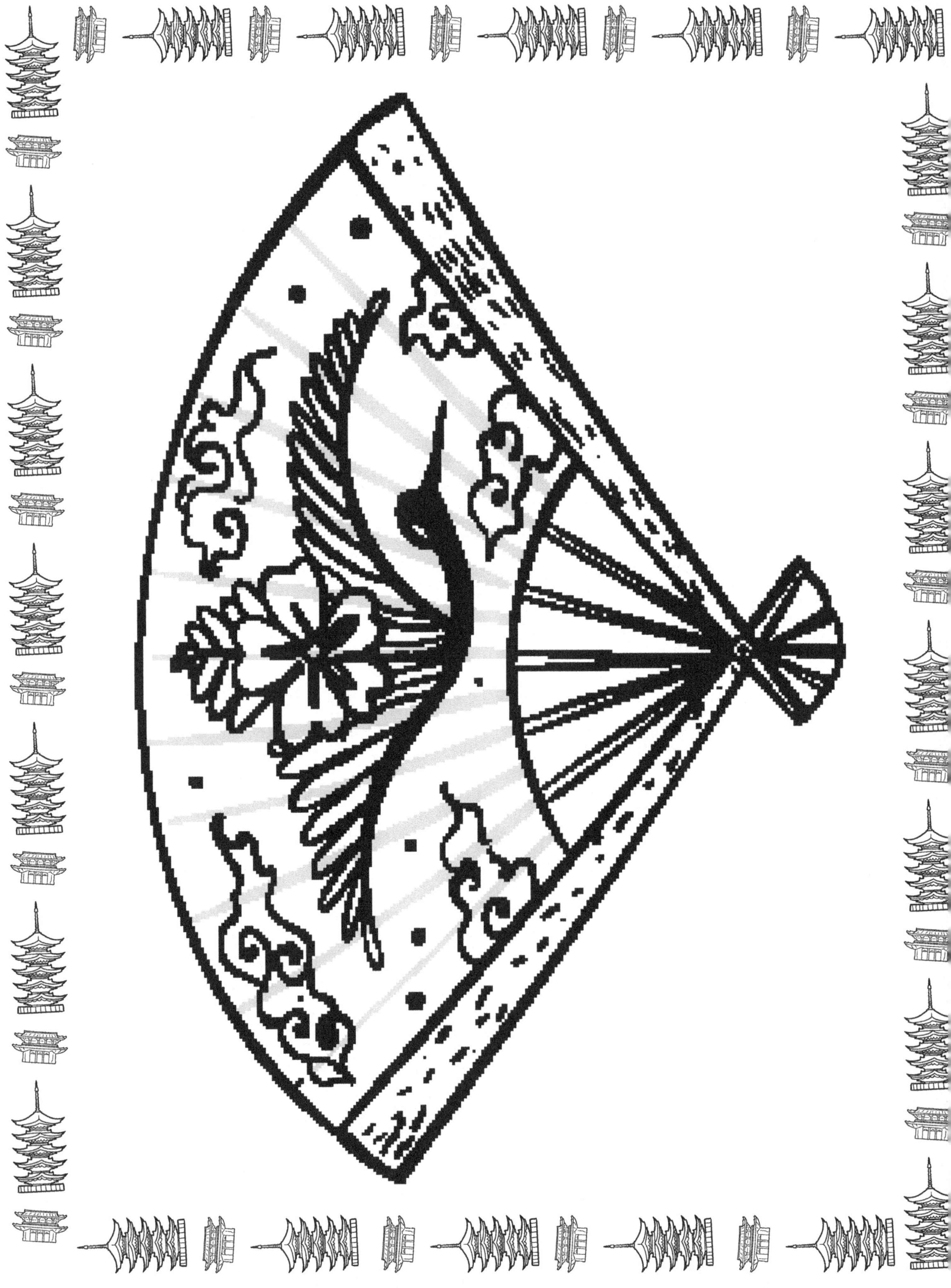

This is a Bleed Through Page If You Are Using a Coloring Marker or Pen!

Bold Illustrations
COLORING BOOKS

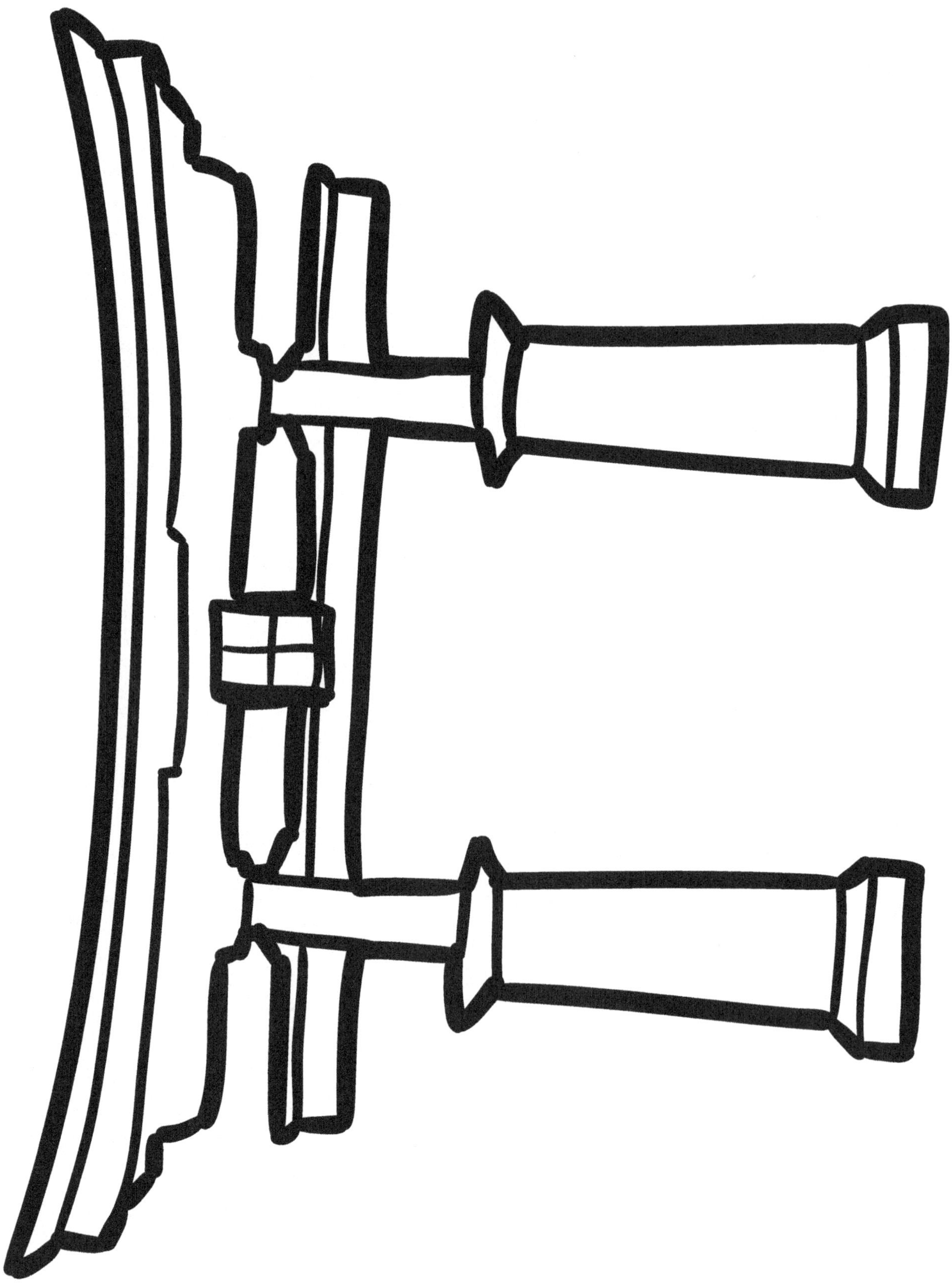

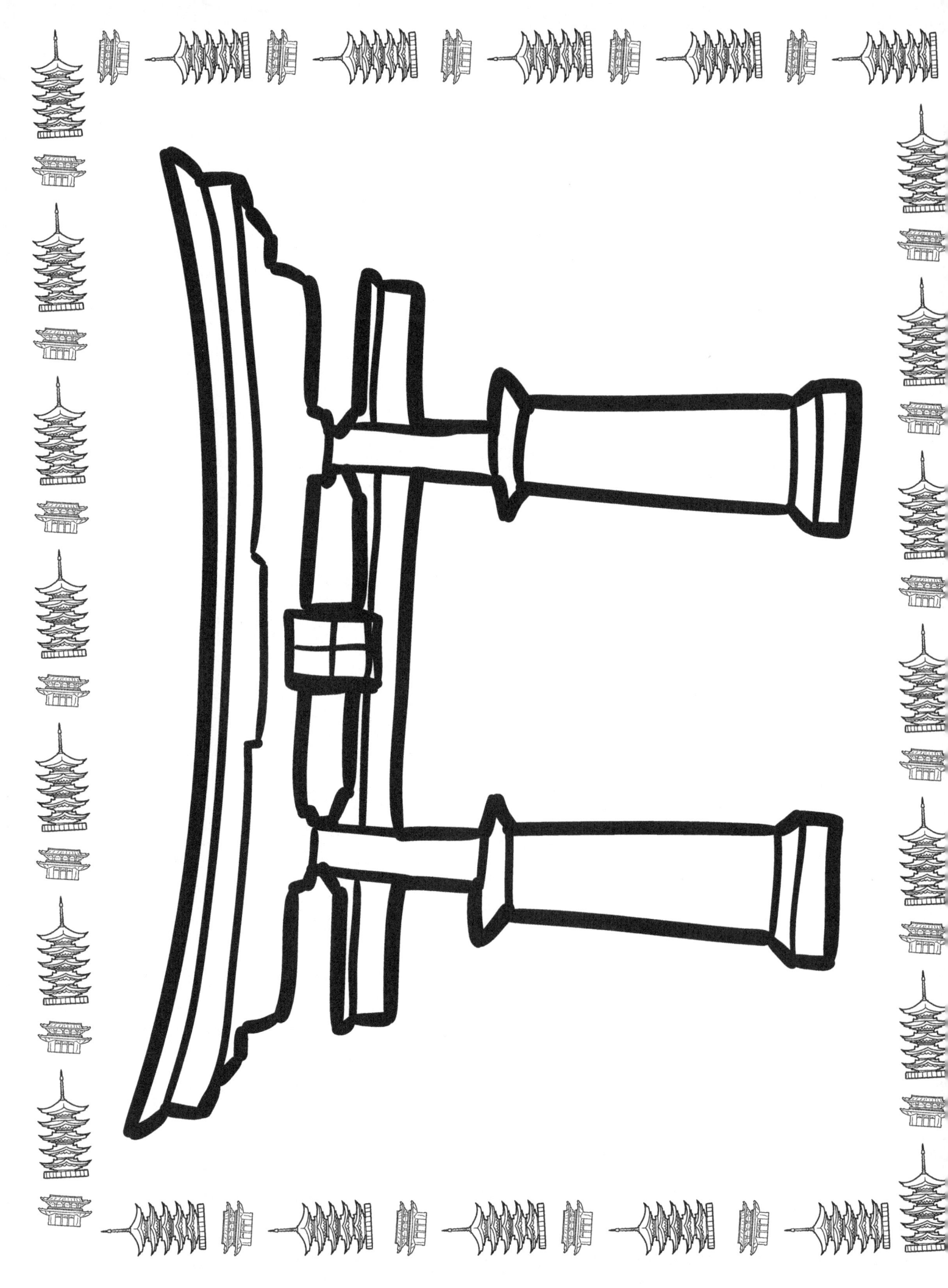

This is a Bleed Through Page If You Are Using a Coloring Marker or Pen!

Bold Illustrations
COLORING BOOKS

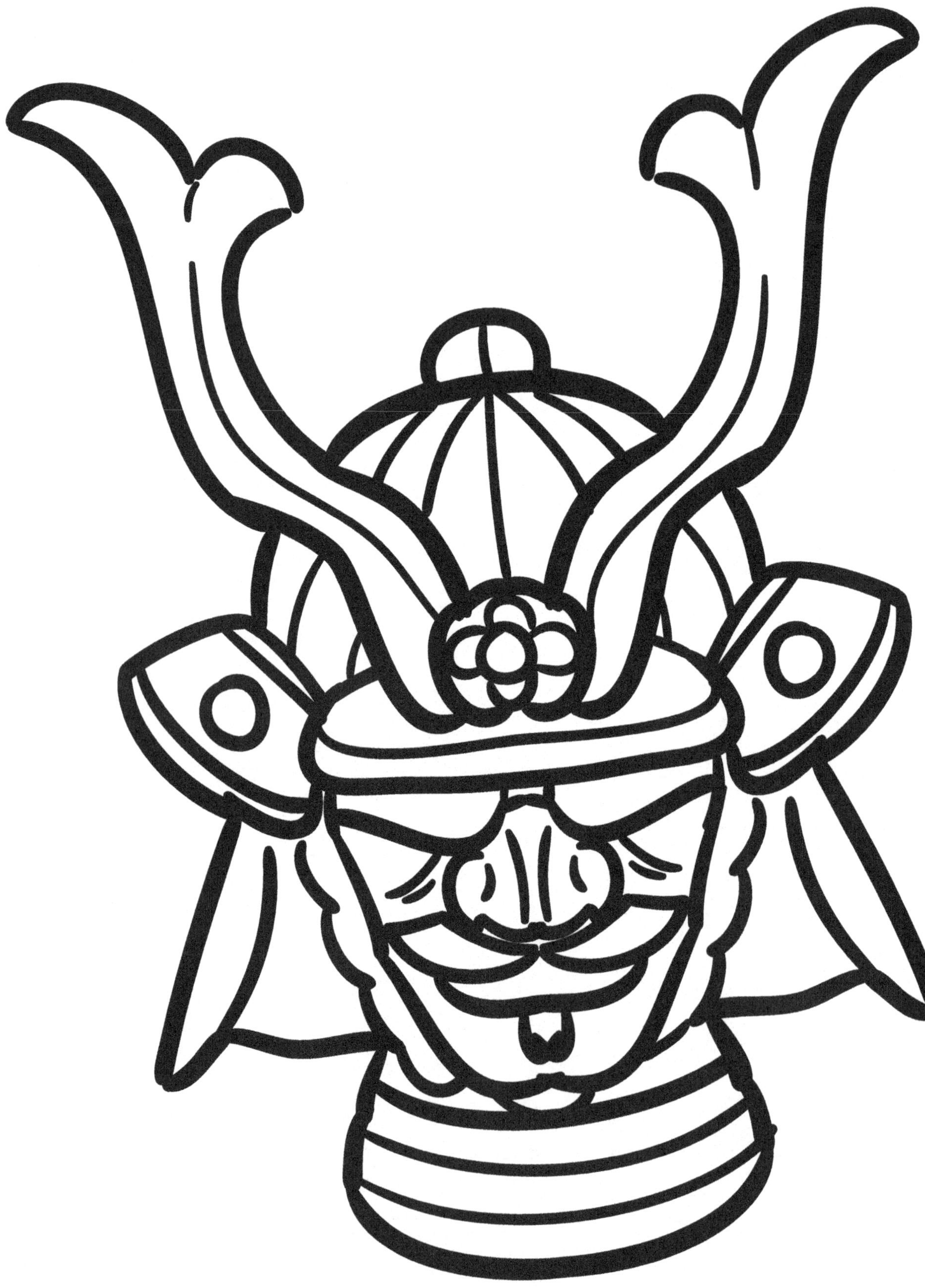

This is a Bleed Through Page If You Are Using a Coloring Marker or Pen!

Bold Illustrations
COLORING BOOKS

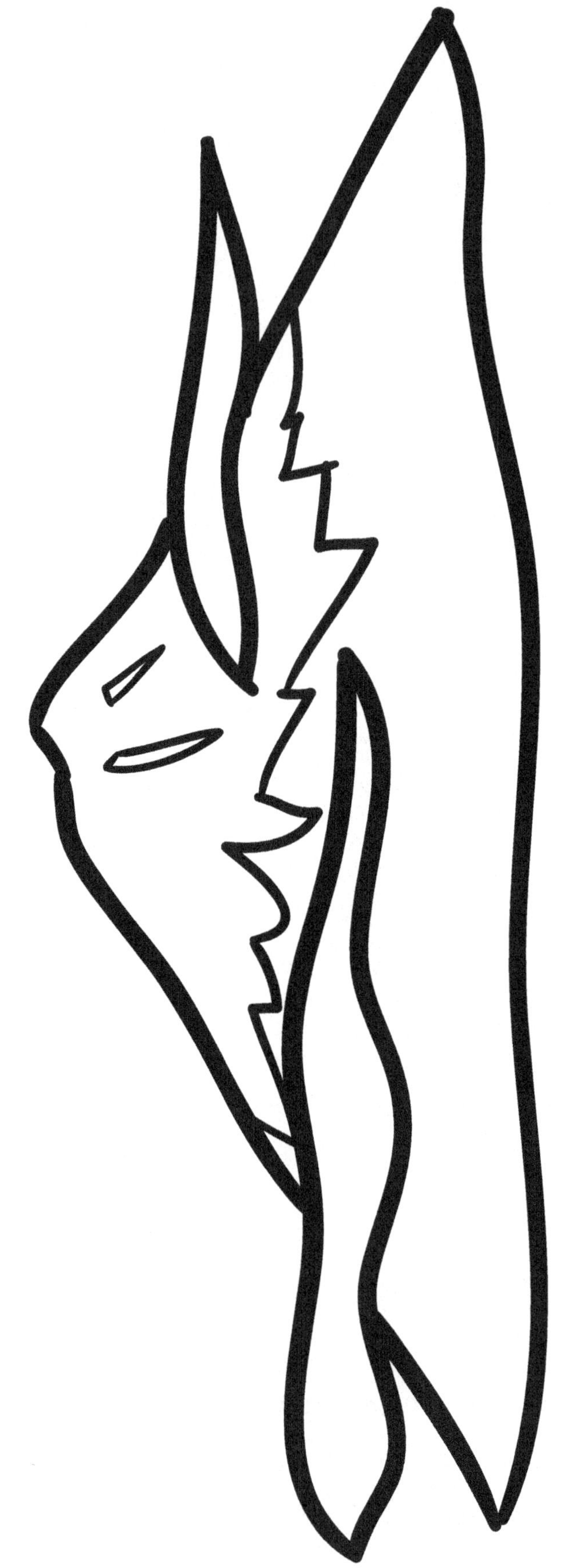

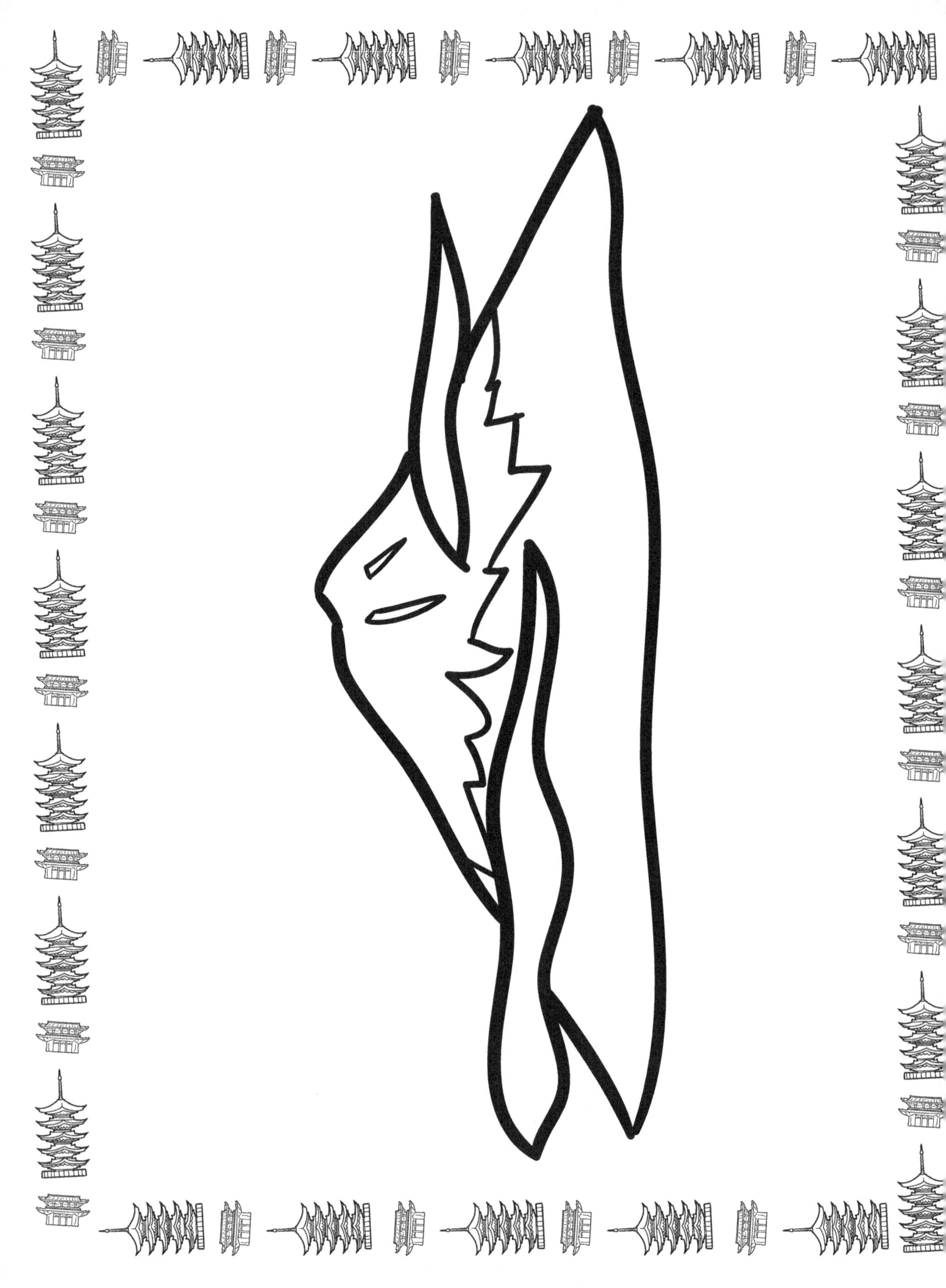

This is a Bleed Through Page If You Are Using a Coloring Marker or Pen!

Bold Illustrations
COLORING BOOKS

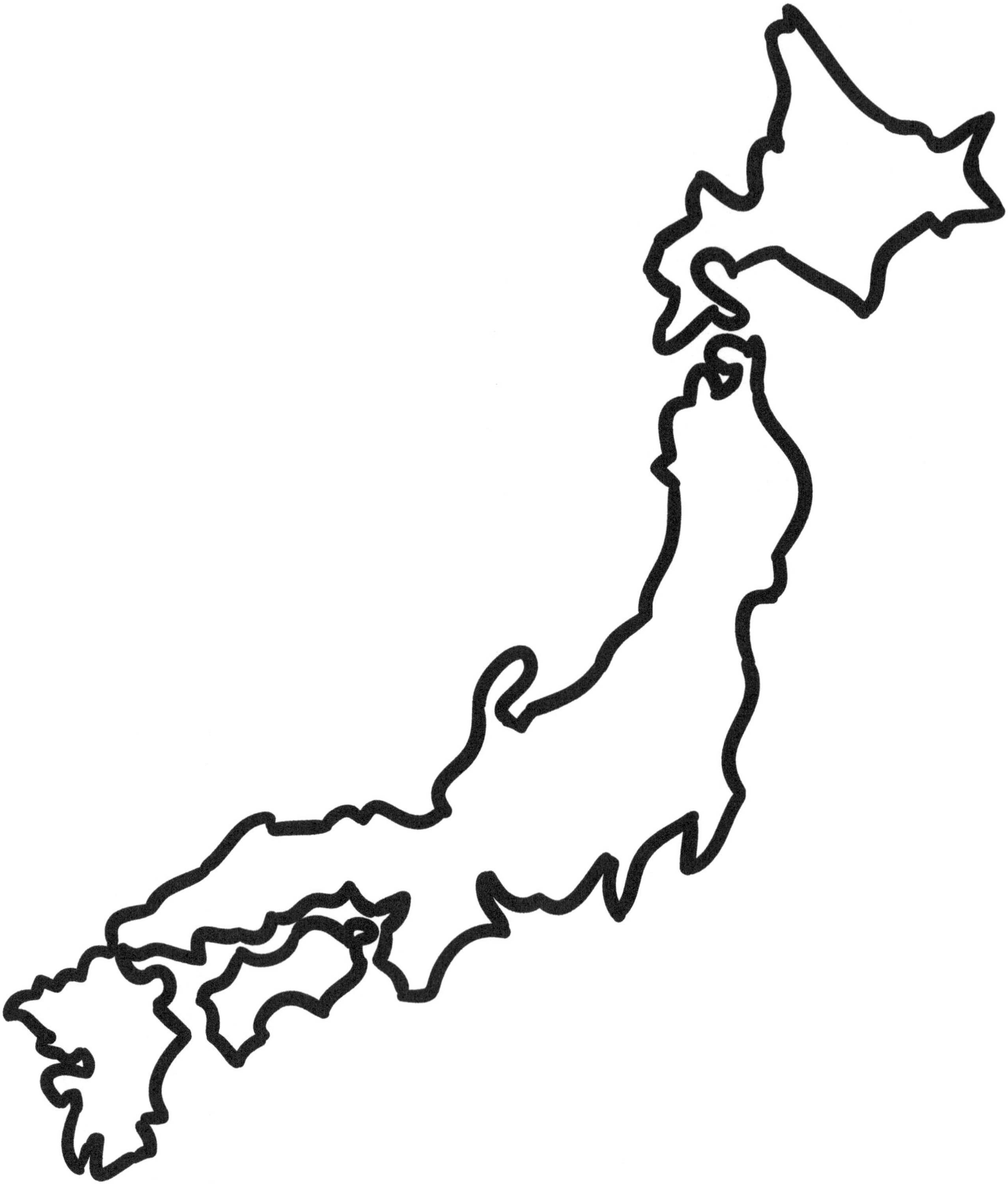

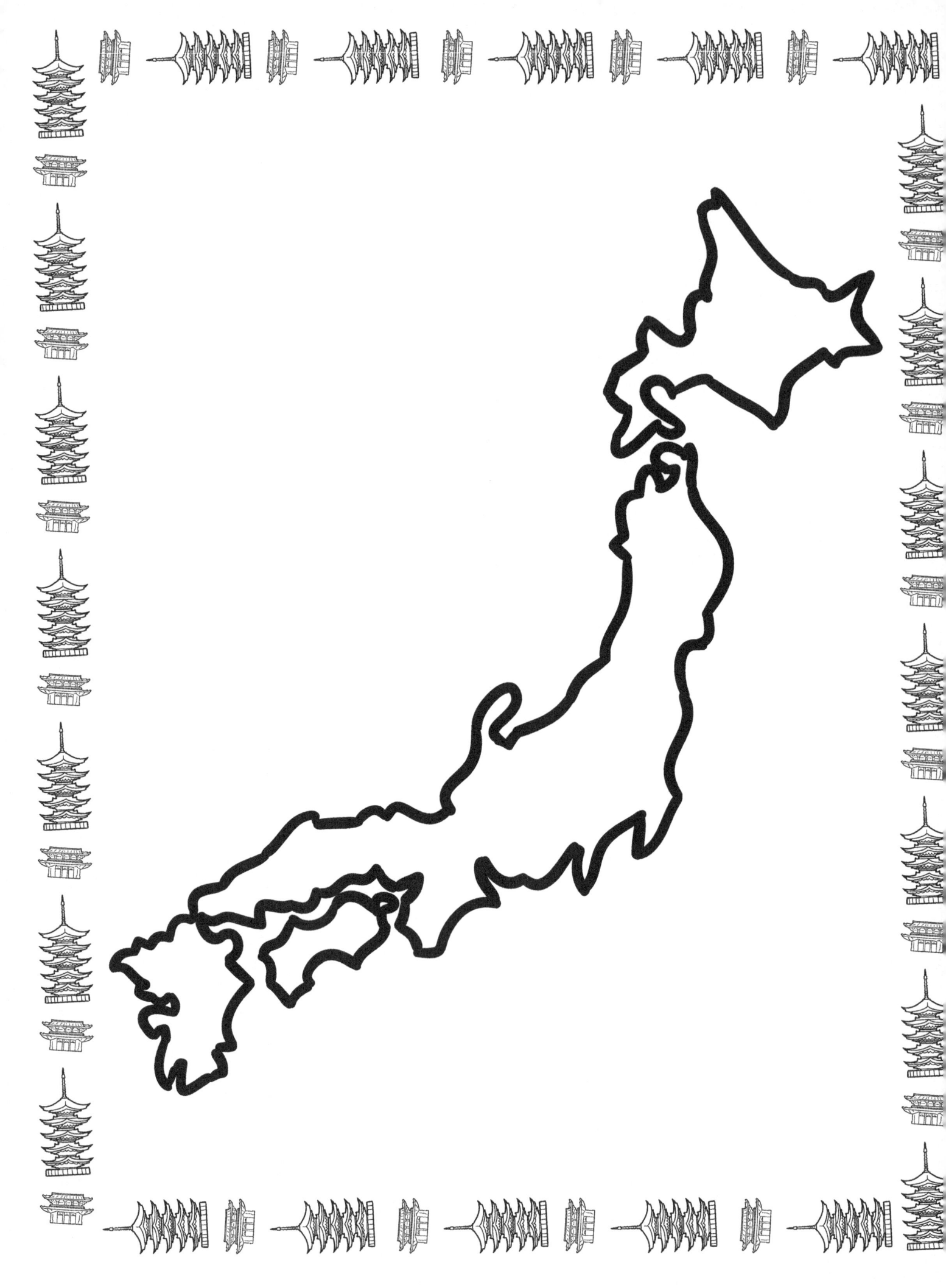

This is a Bleed Through Page If You Are Using a Coloring Marker or Pen!

Bold Illustrations
COLORING BOOKS

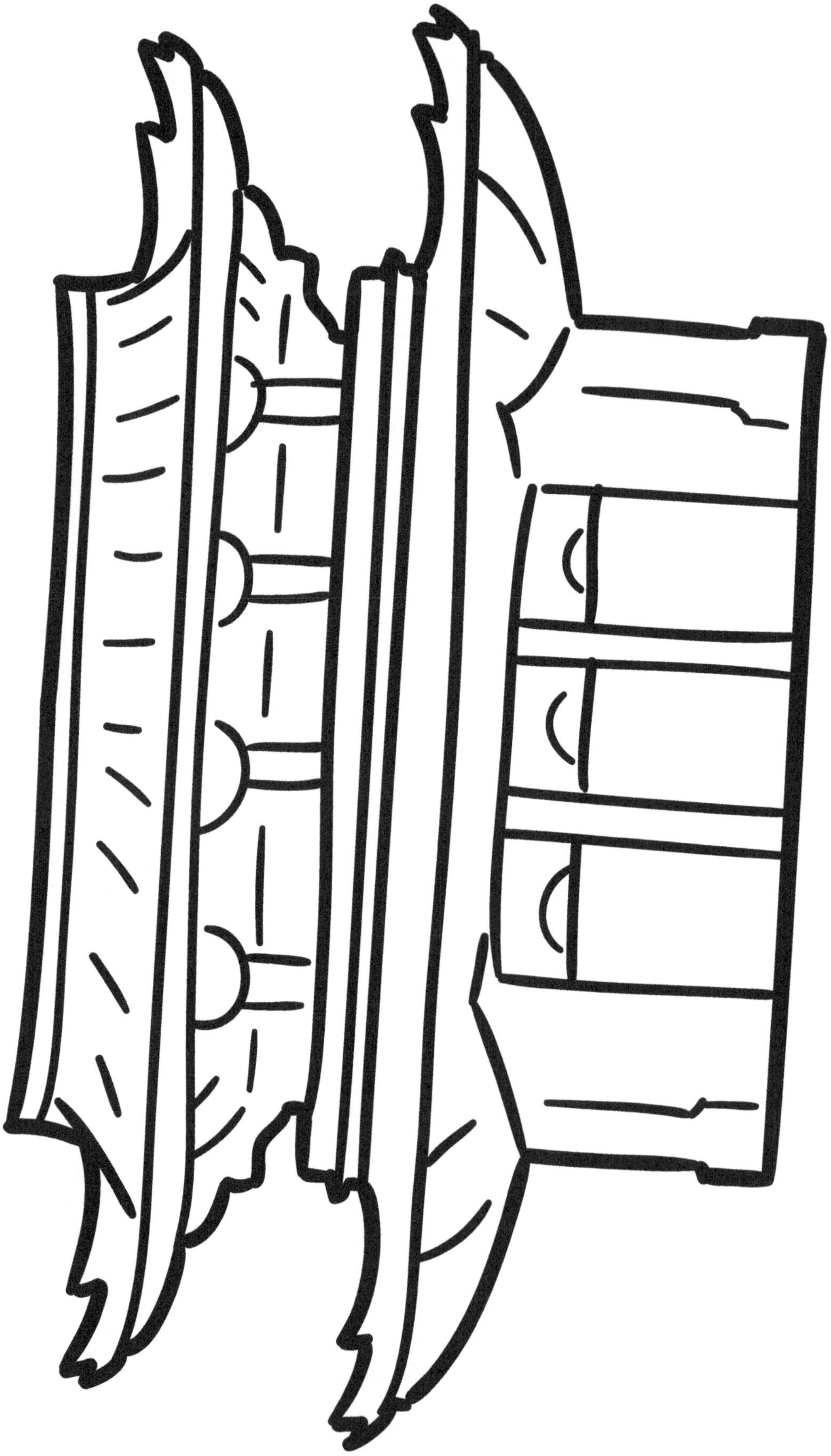

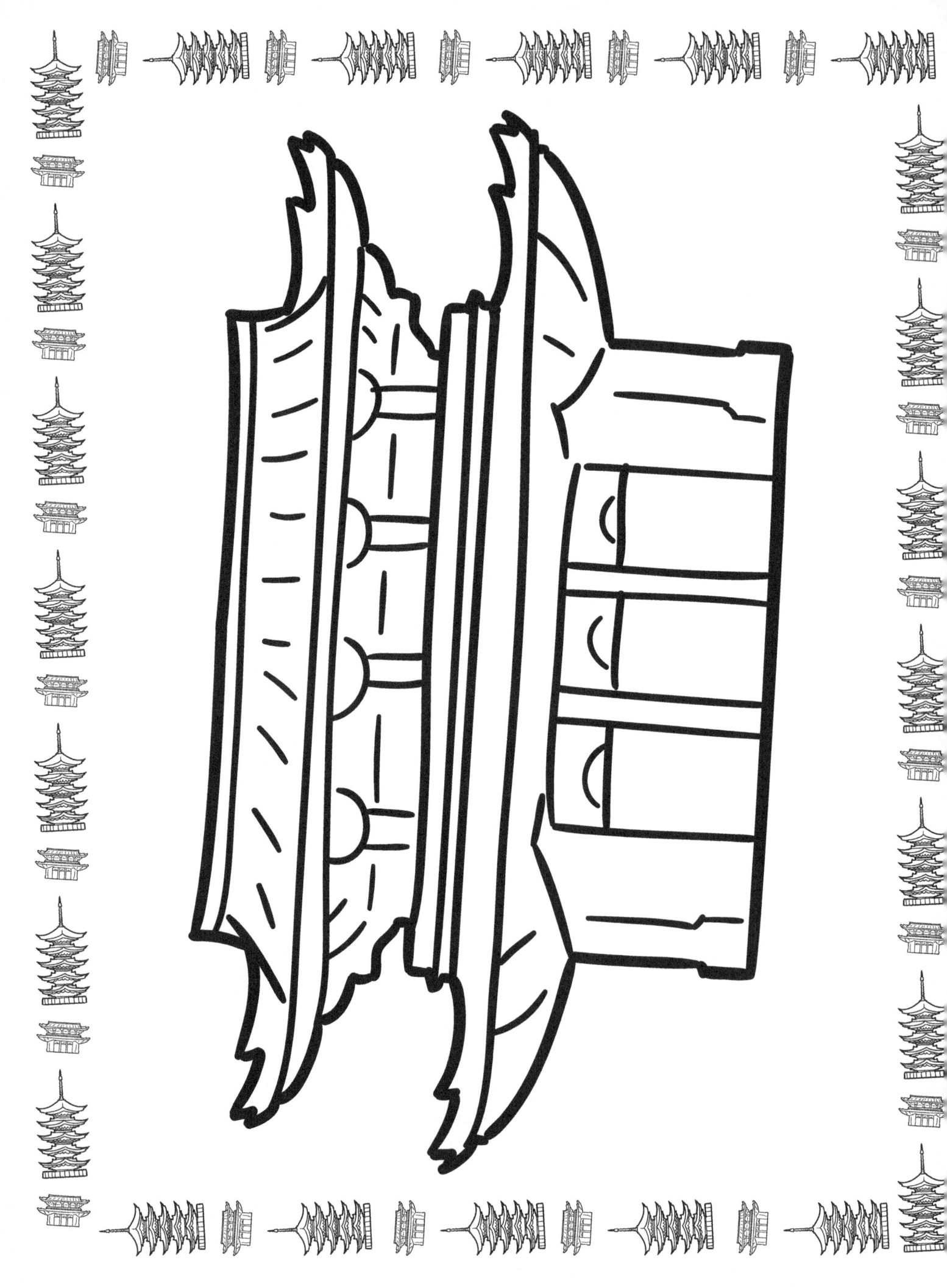

This is a Bleed Through Page If You Are Using a Coloring Marker or Pen!

Bold Illustrations
COLORING BOOKS

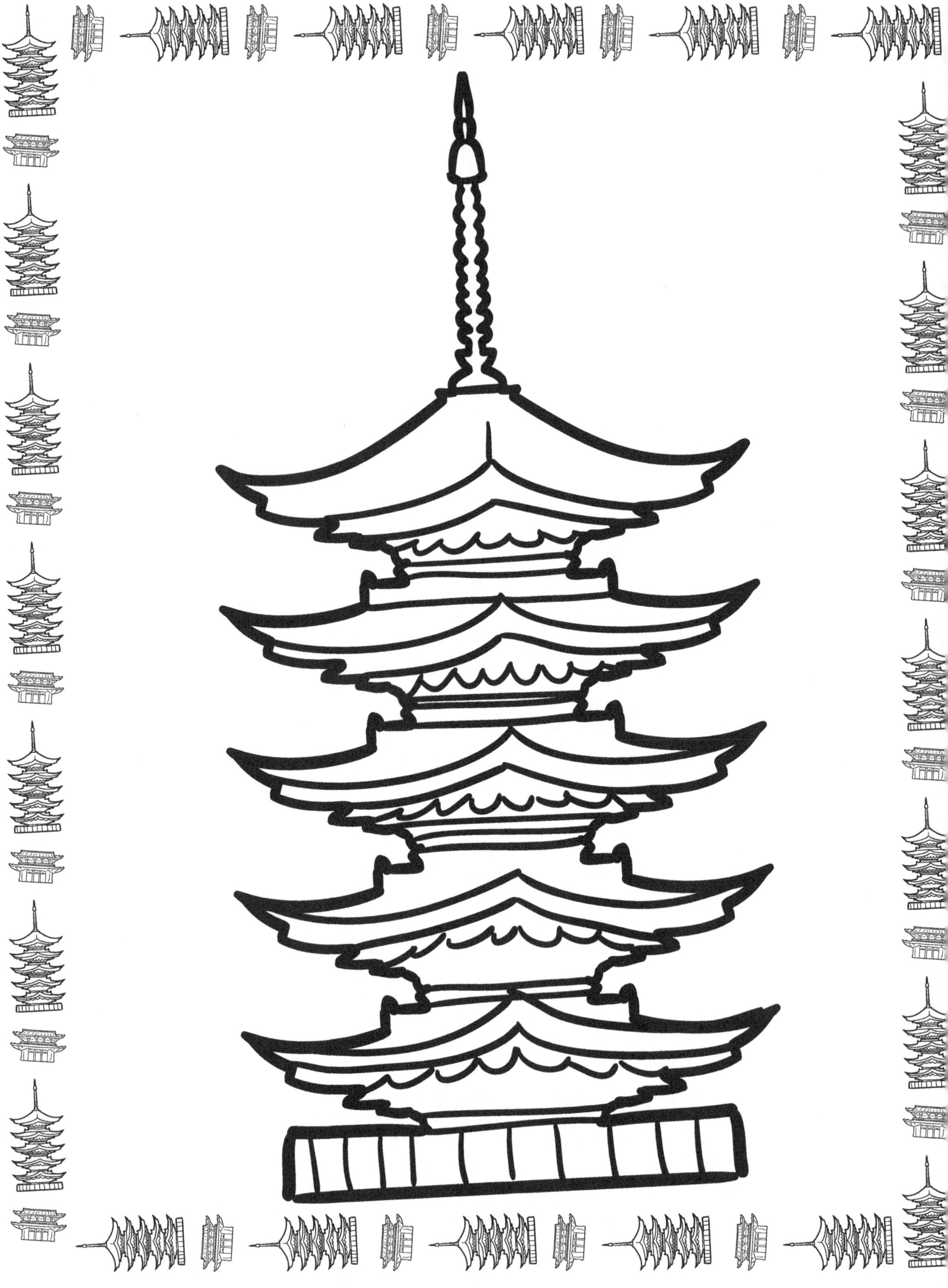

This is a Bleed Through Page If You Are Using a Coloring Marker or Pen!

Bold Illustrations
COLORING BOOKS

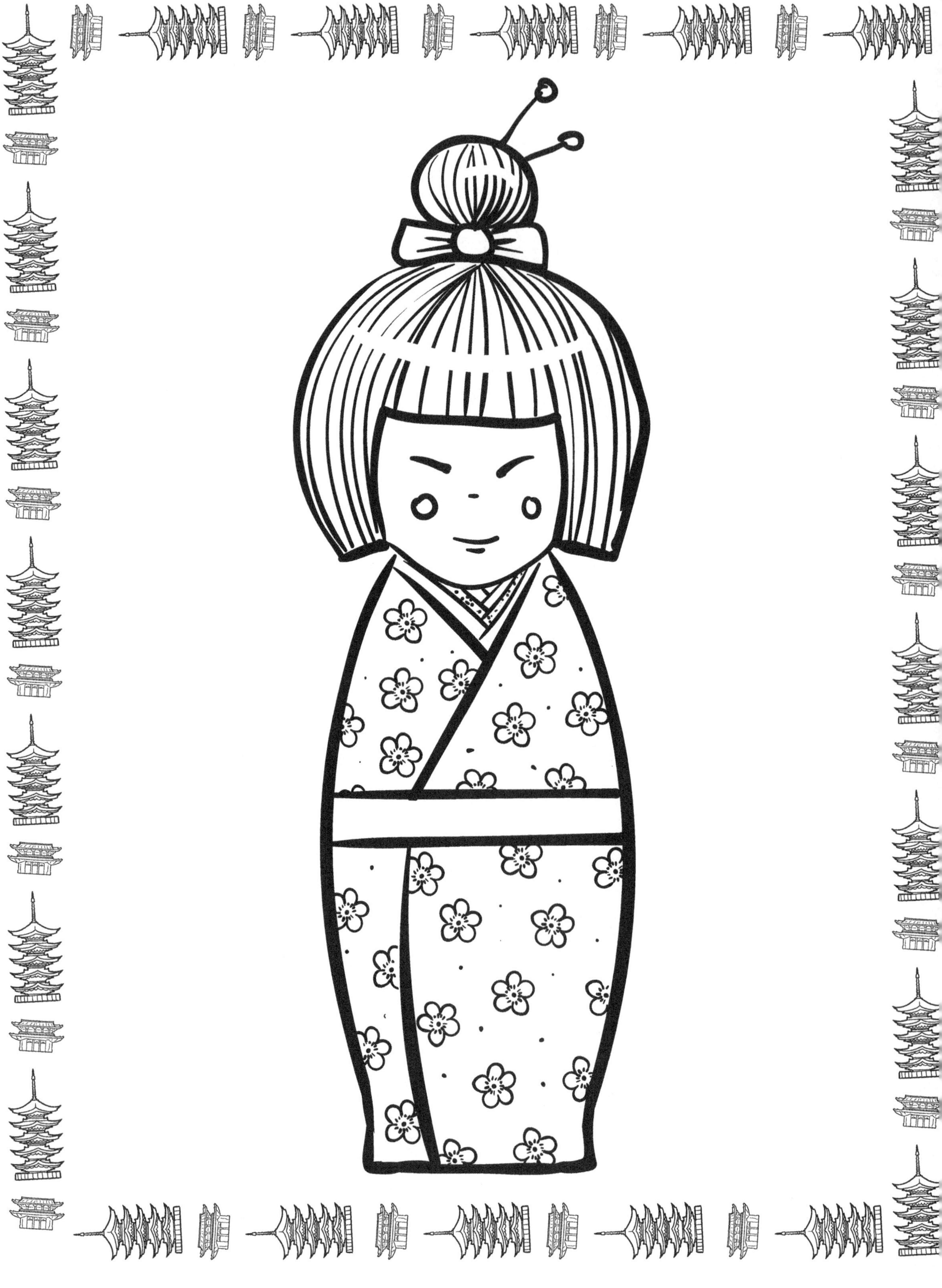

This is a Bleed Through Page If You Are Using a Coloring Marker or Pen!

Bold Illustrations
COLORING BOOKS

禅

This is a Bleed Through Page If You Are Using a Coloring Marker or Pen!

Bold Illustrations
COLORING BOOKS

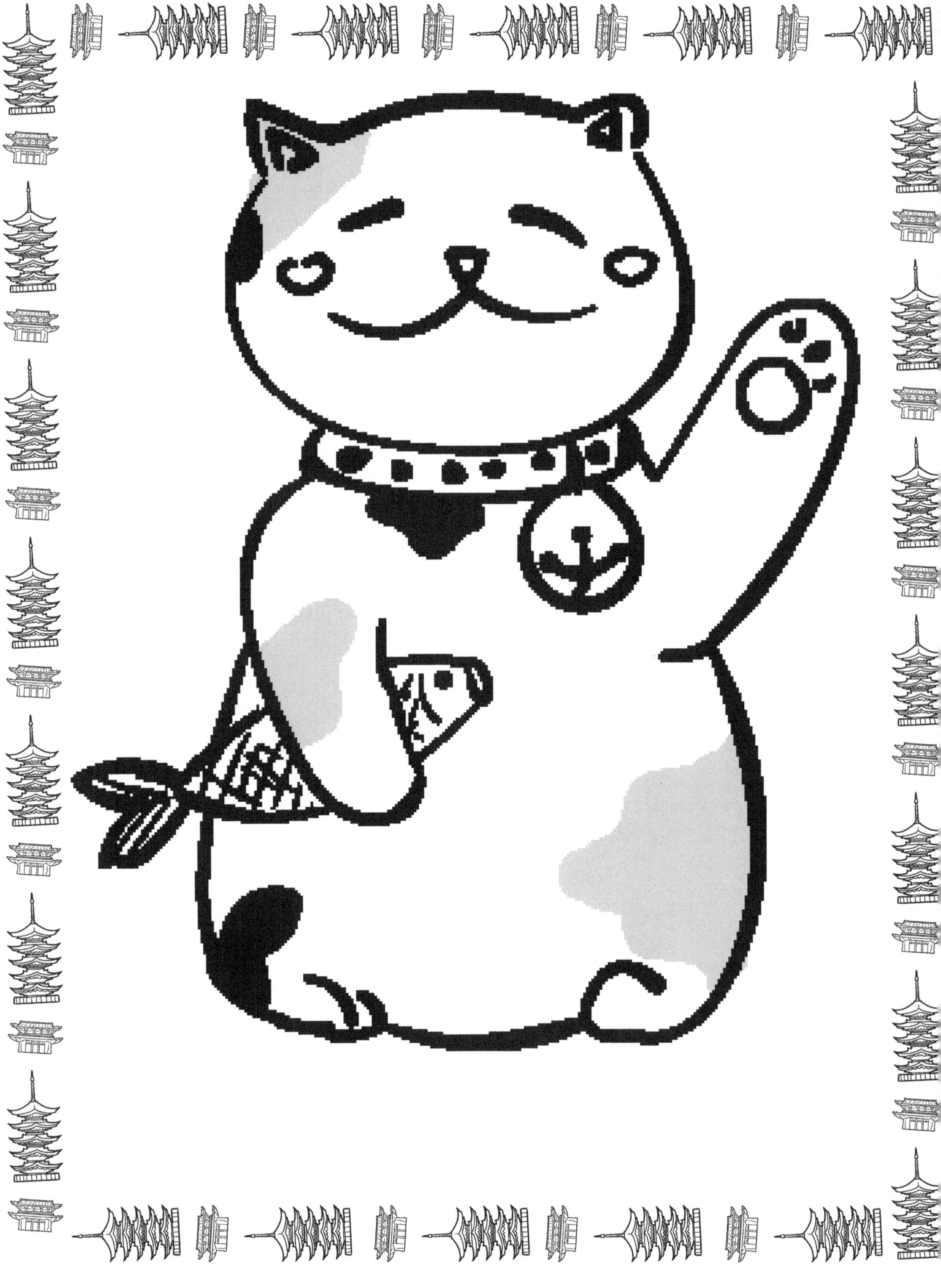

This is a Bleed Through Page If You Are Using a Coloring Marker or Pen!

Bold Illustrations
COLORING BOOKS

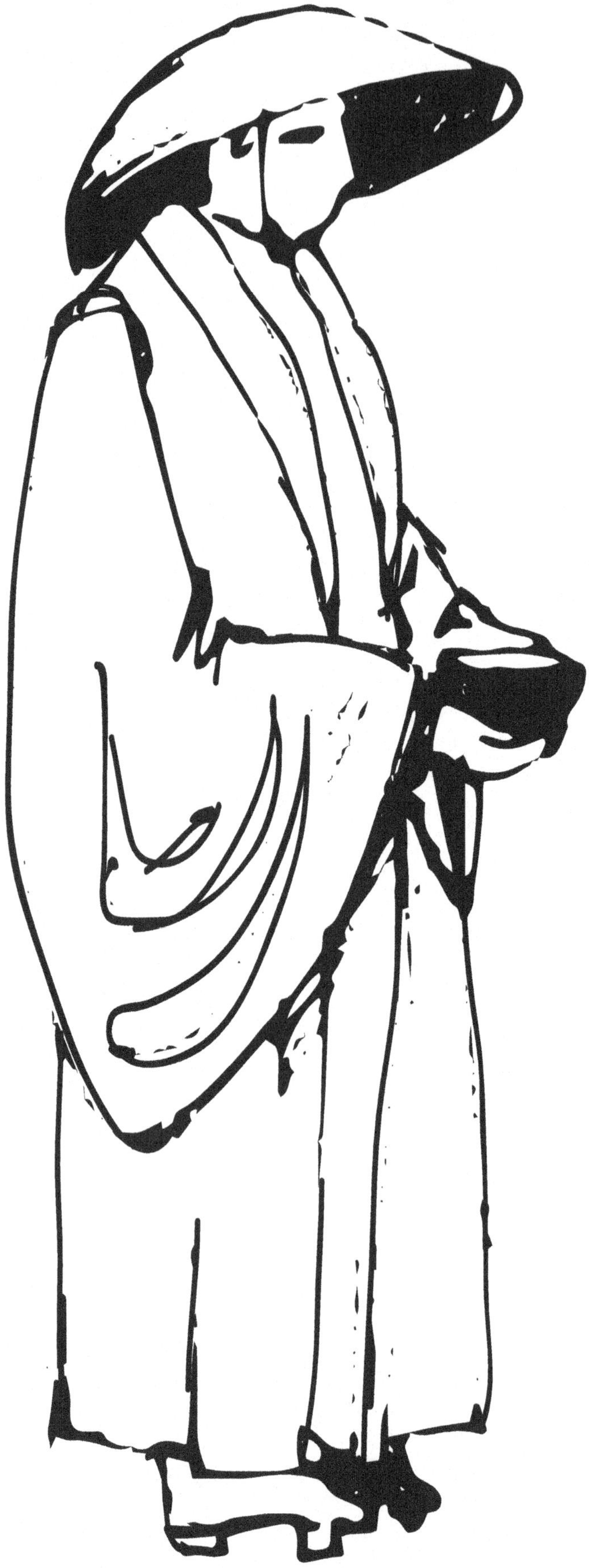

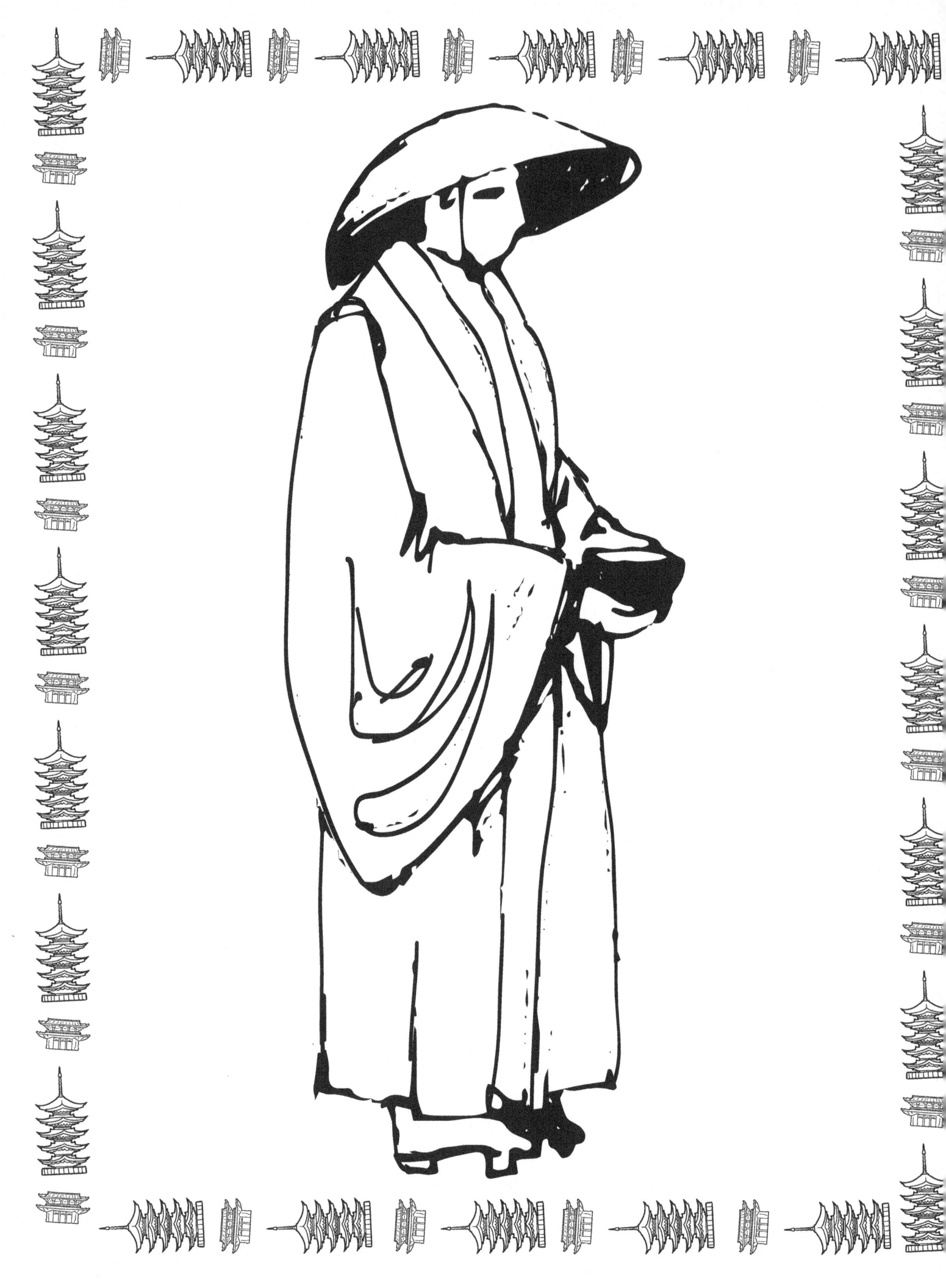

This is a Bleed Through Page If You Are Using a Coloring Marker or Pen!

Bold Illustrations
COLORING BOOKS

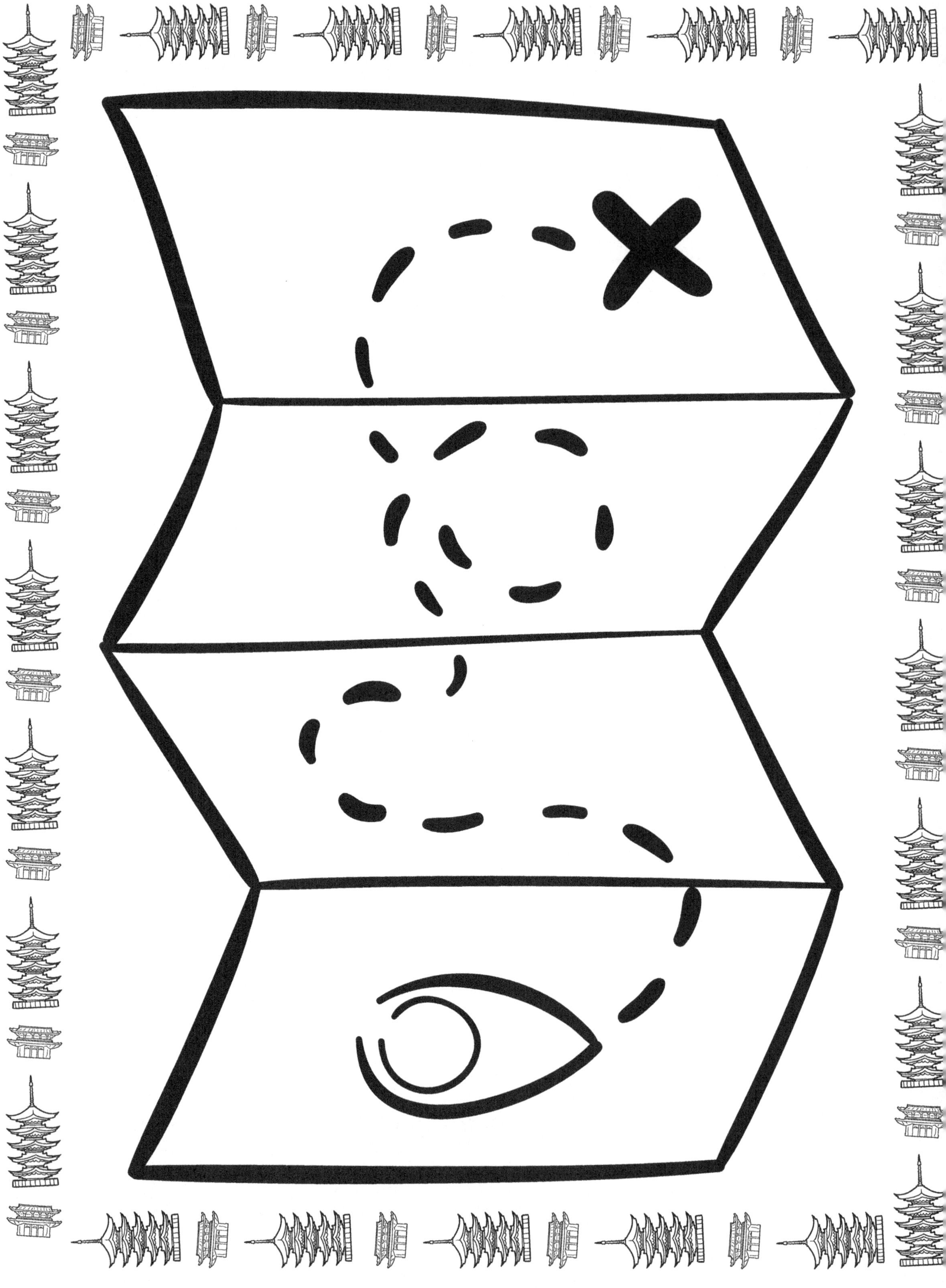

This is a Bleed Through Page If You Are Using a Coloring Marker or Pen!

Bold Illustrations
COLORING BOOKS

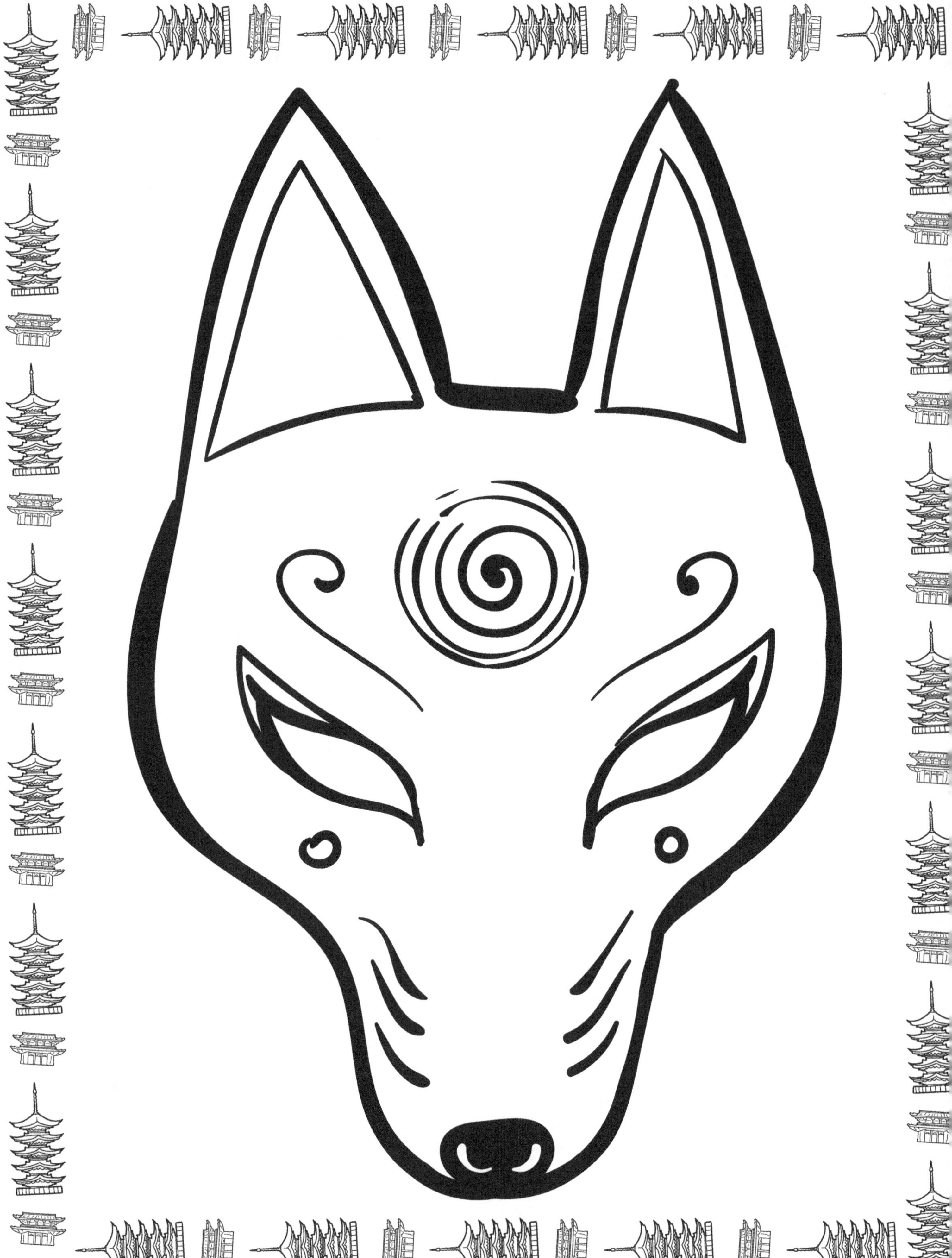

This is a Bleed Through Page If You Are Using a Coloring Marker or Pen!

Bold Illustrations
COLORING BOOKS

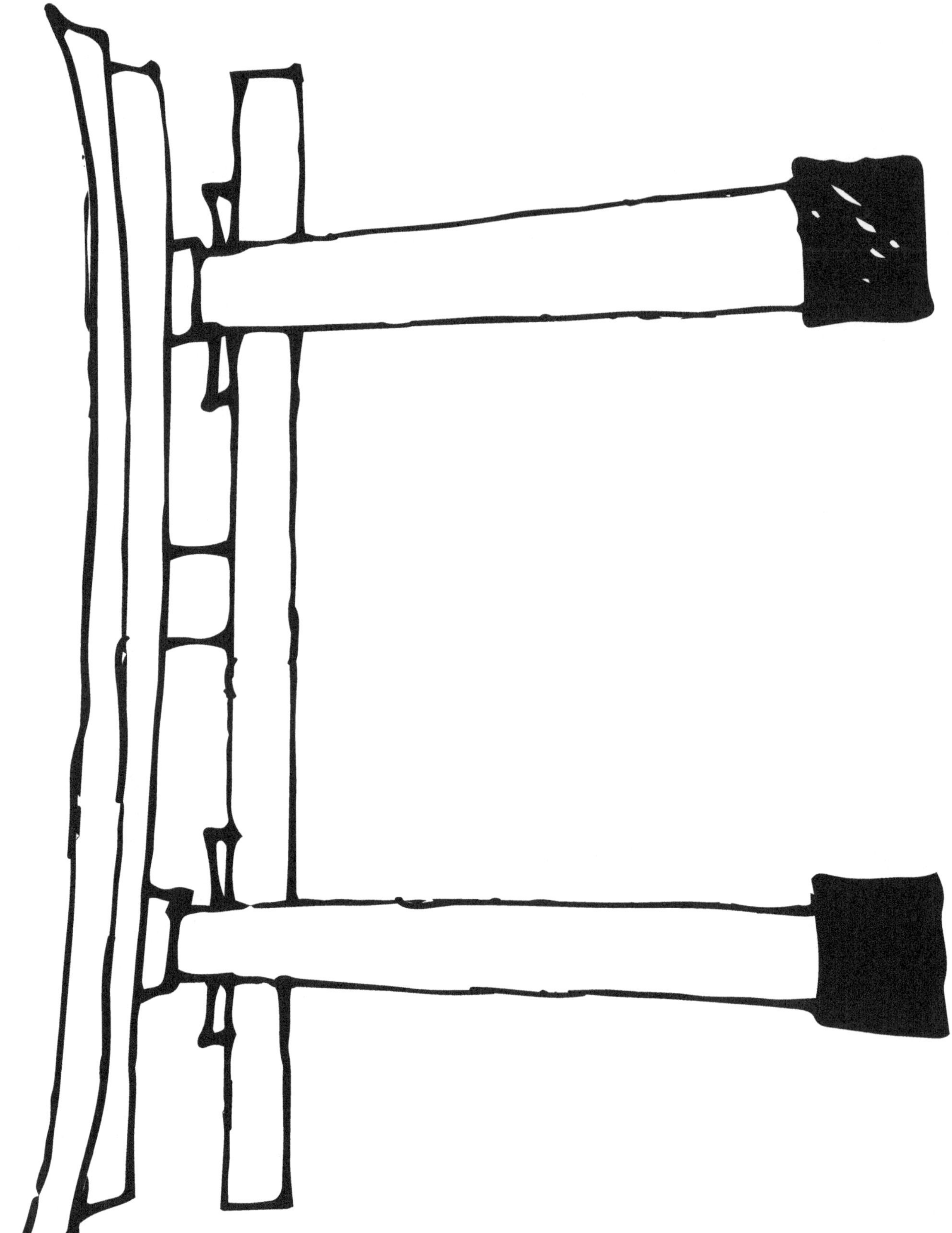

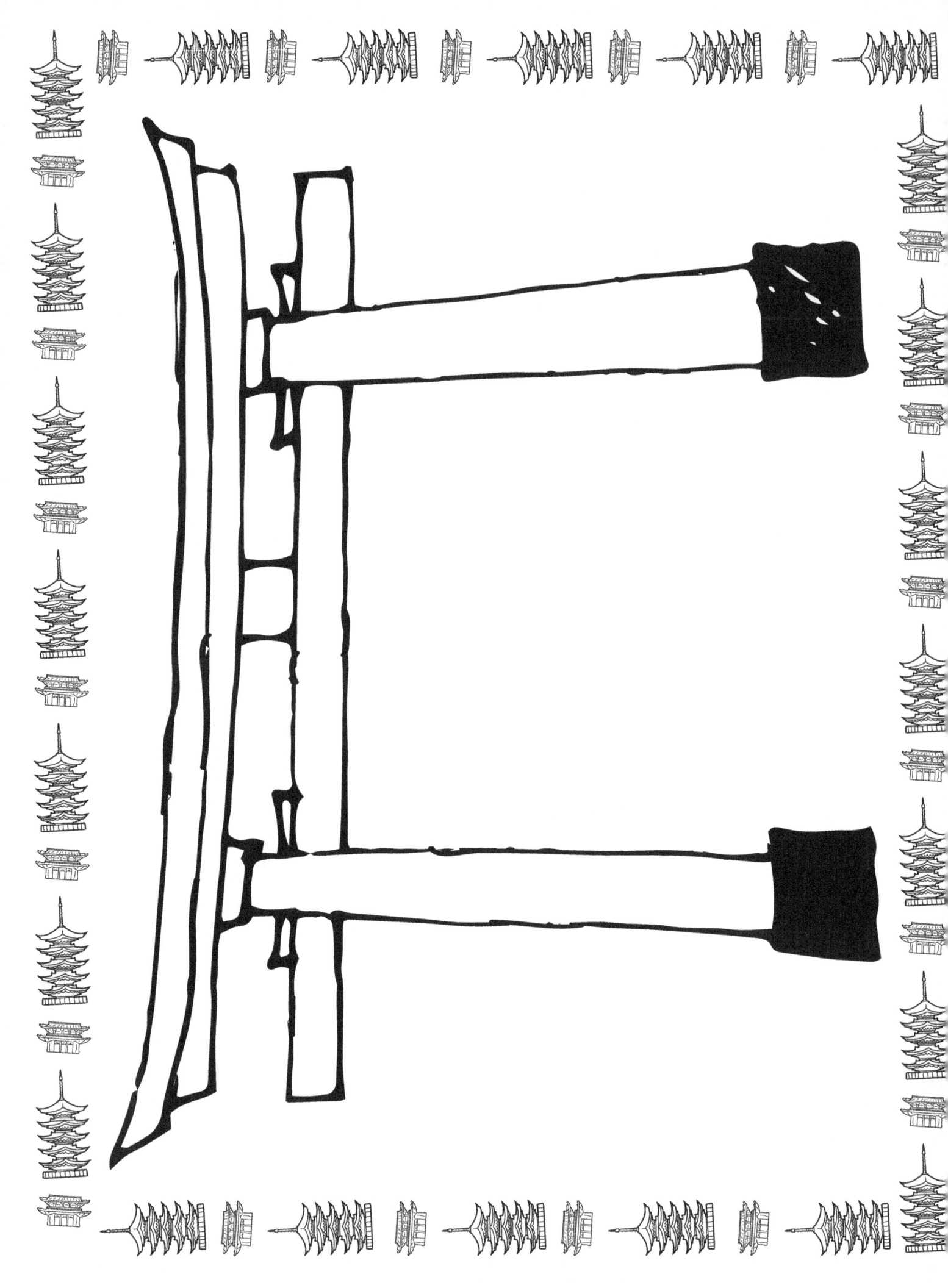

This is a Bleed Through Page If You Are Using a Coloring Marker or Pen!

Bold Illustrations
COLORING BOOKS

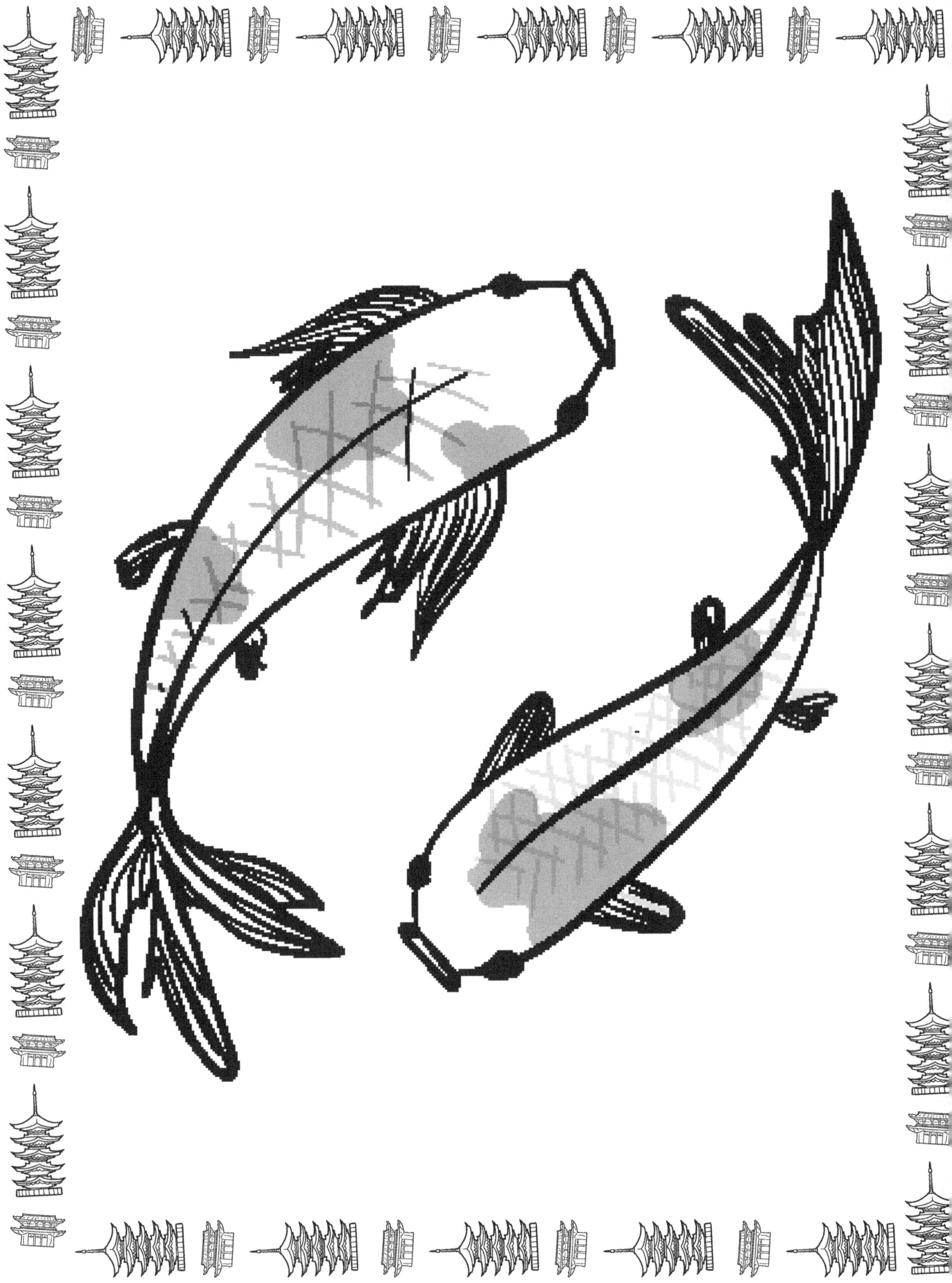

This is a Bleed Through Page If You Are Using a Coloring Marker or Pen!

Bold Illustrations
COLORING BOOKS

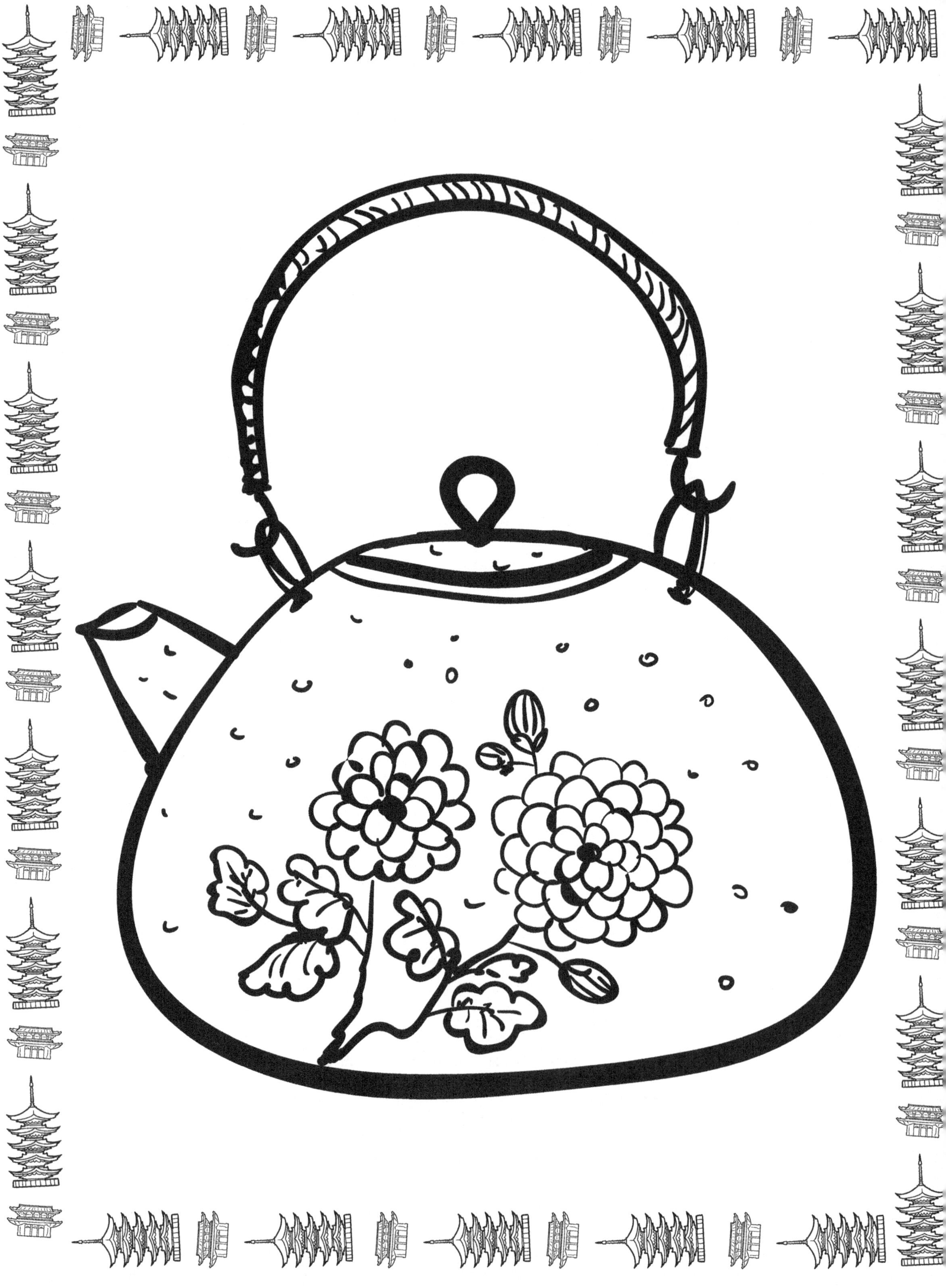

This is a Bleed Through Page If You Are Using a Coloring Marker or Pen!

Bold Illustrations
COLORING BOOKS

This is a Bleed Through Page If You Are Using a Coloring Marker or Pen!

Bold Illustrations
COLORING BOOKS

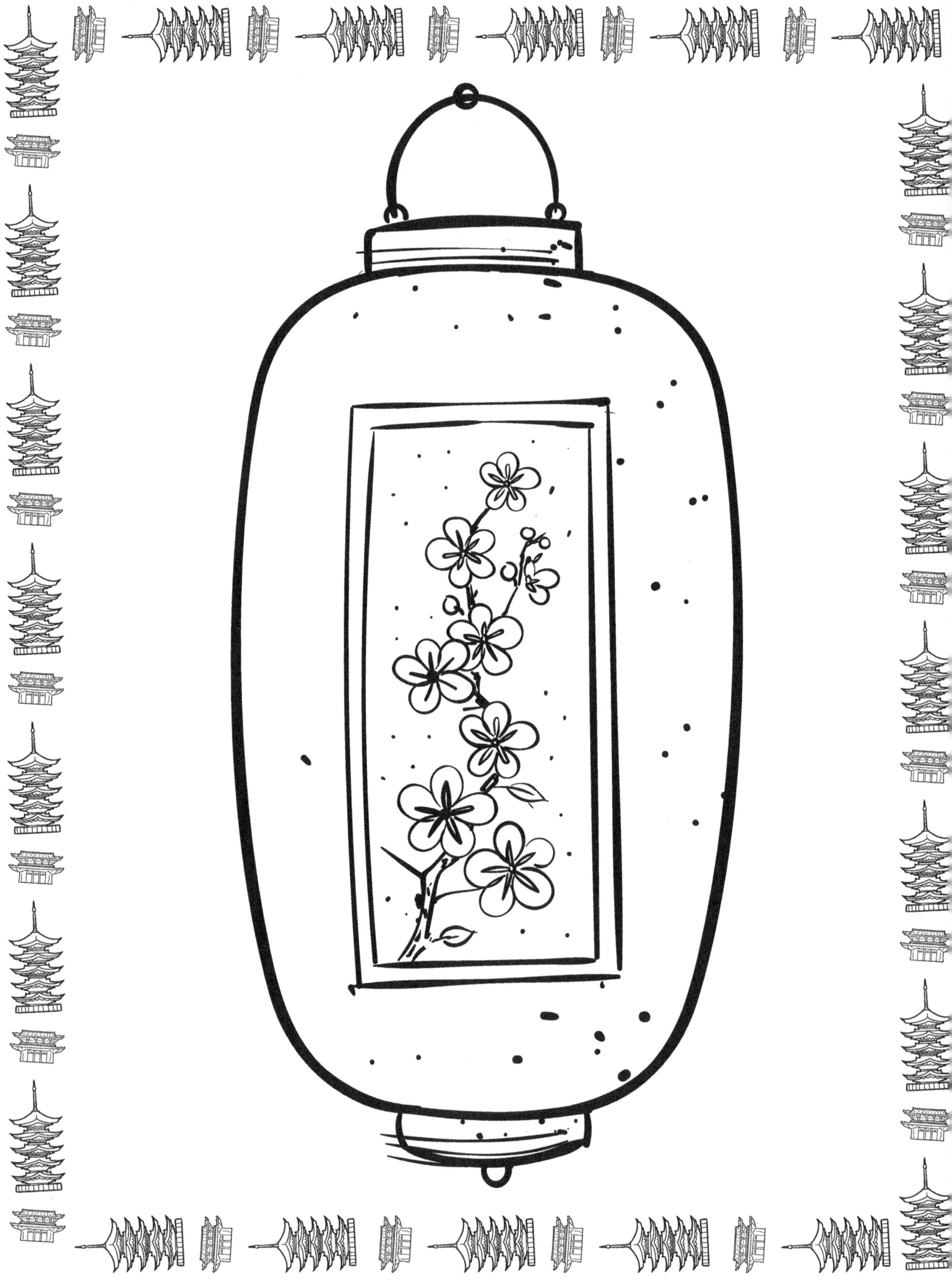

This is a Bleed Through Page If You Are Using a Coloring Marker or Pen!

Bold Illustrations
COLORING BOOKS

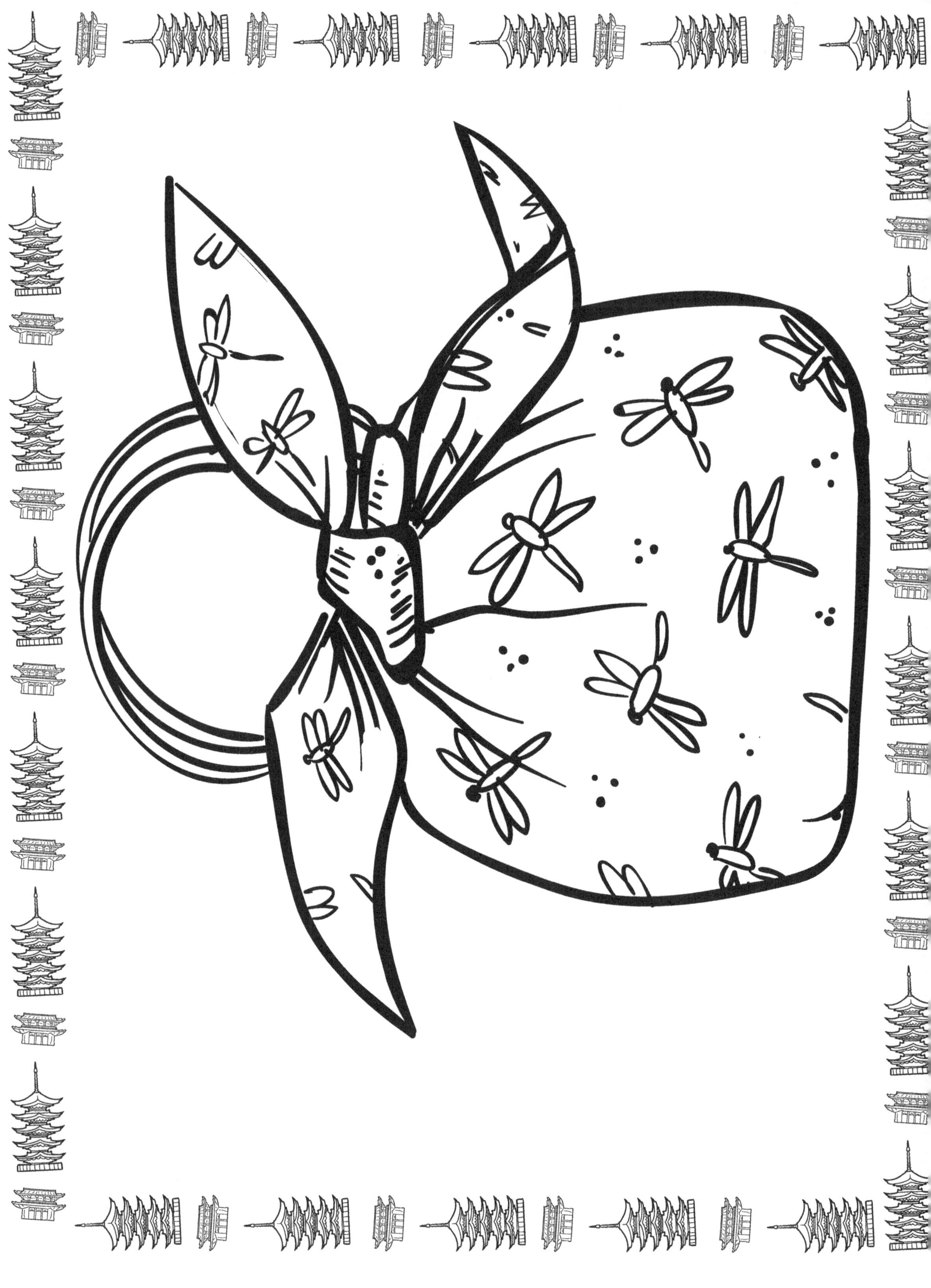

This is a Bleed Through Page If You Are Using a Coloring Marker or Pen!

Bold Illustrations
COLORING BOOKS

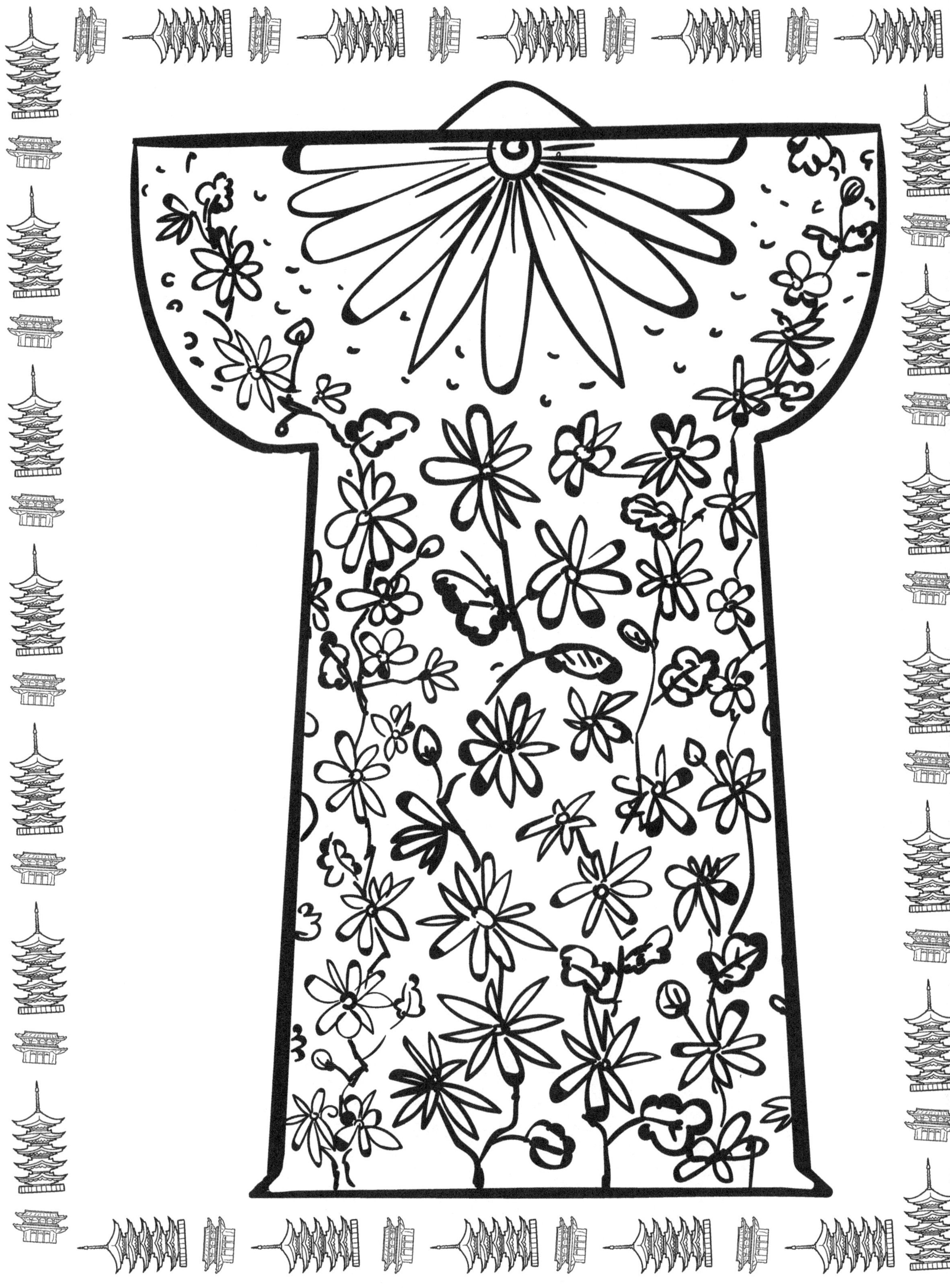

This is a Bleed Through Page If You Are Using a Coloring Marker or Pen!

Bold Illustrations
COLORING BOOKS

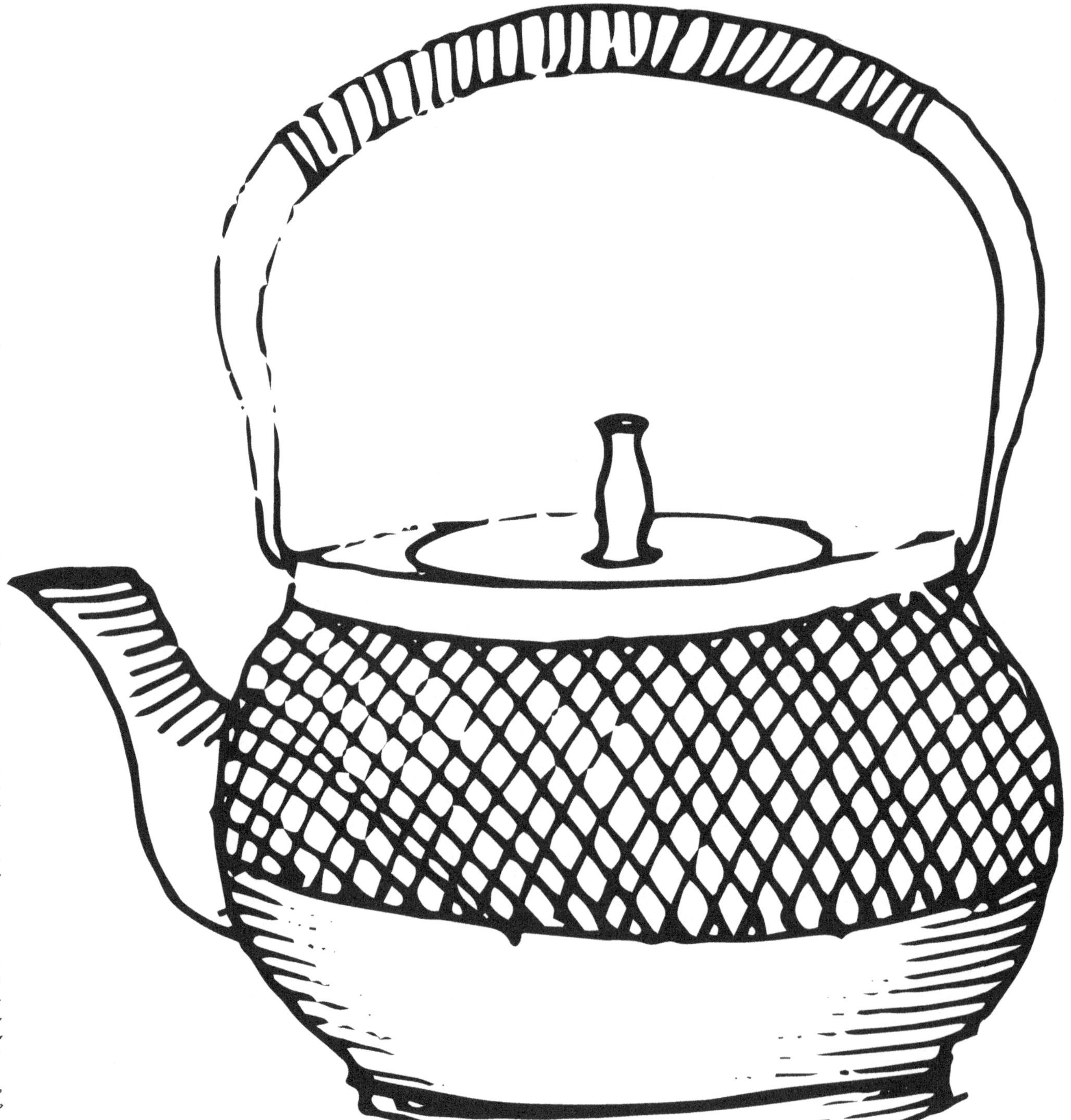

This is a Bleed Through Page If You Are Using a Coloring Marker or Pen!

Bold Illustrations
COLORING BOOKS

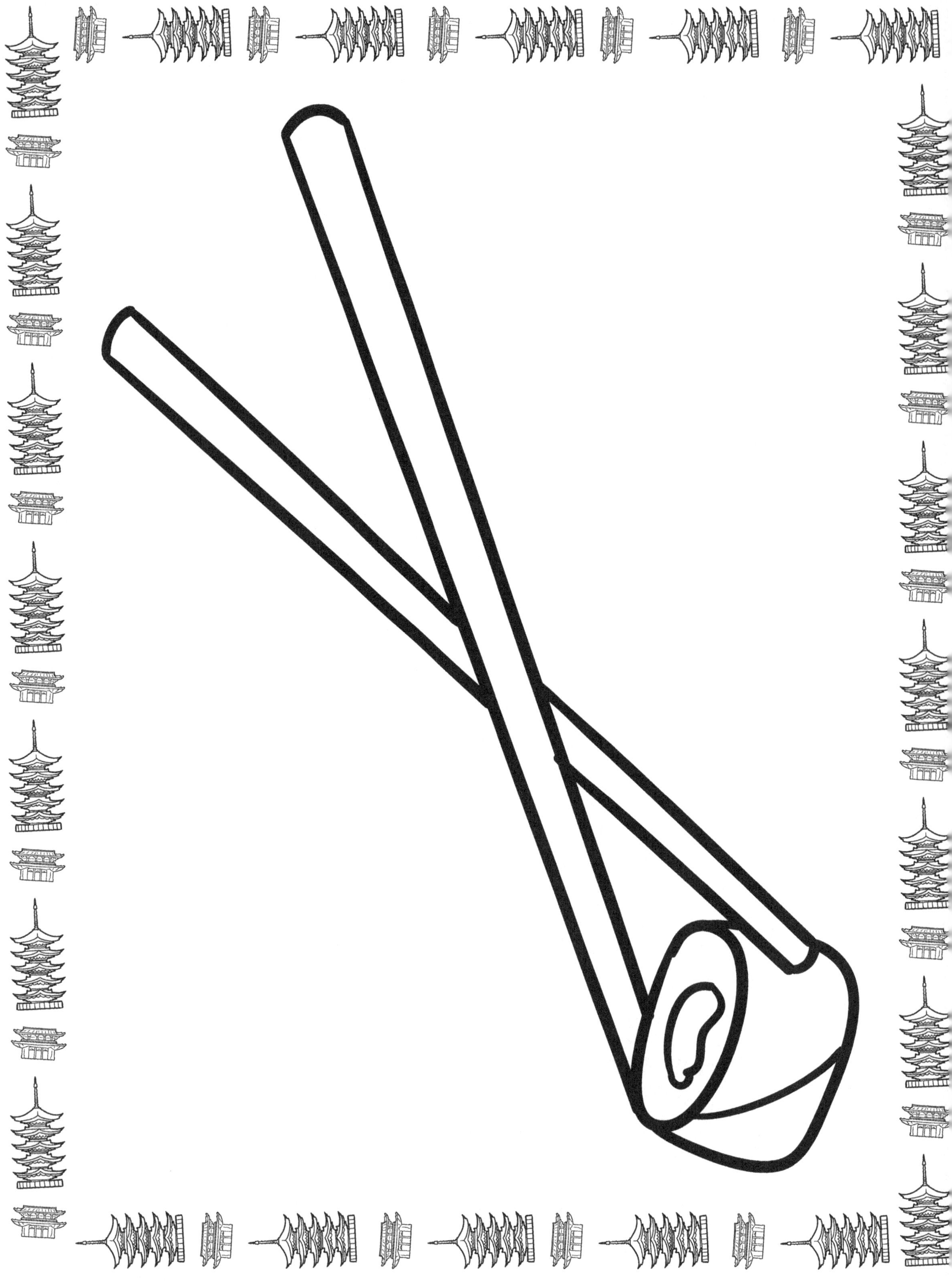

This is a Bleed Through Page If You Are Using a Coloring Marker or Pen!

Bold Illustrations
COLORING BOOKS

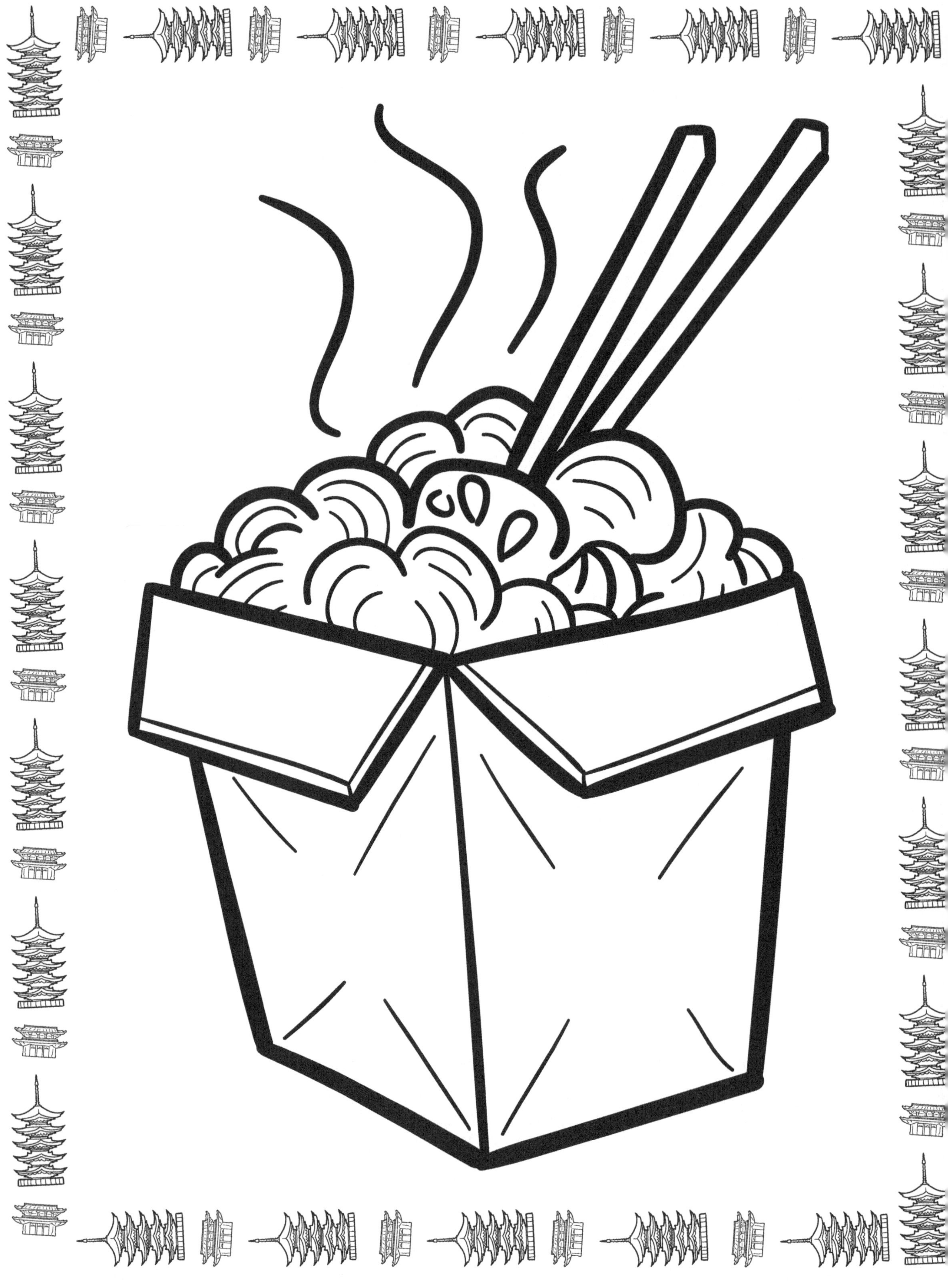

Made in the USA
Monee, IL
18 November 2020